IF
Woods

## About the Author

First Things First, Fictional love and life resembles reality. It is imperative for me to show how the Lord meets individuals where they are and restores them through His Word for them to become the individuals he predestined them to be.

I am a believer in Jesus Christ, who is the lover of my soul, so much that He gave His life that mine might be saved from eternal damnation. Therefore, His praises shall continually be on my lips. I give Him Glory & Honor for they belong to Him.

I am happily married to a wonderful and handsome man who supports me in all things. He encourages me to stand on the promise that I can do all things through Christ that strengthens me. He is a solid rock, my muse, the second lover of my soul, and the only lover of my body. I adore him. Song of Solomon 3:4, explains how I adore him, by stating "but I found him whom my soul loveth: I held him, and would not let him go." That is Biblical Romance read it for yourself.

Our union has been blessed with two handsome sons, one beautiful daughter, and a Shi-Tzu (dog) we all love and think he is more human than Shi-Tzu.

I have been called to narrate Christian love stories that reflect the greatest love of all time. That love is Christ's love for his bride, the church.

The characters that live these stories do not always start on the right path. Sometimes they fall down, but through the long-suffering of the Heavenly Father and their earthly lovers, they find redemption and happiness (in most cases).

Love is patient! Love is Kind!

## Acknowledgments

**Readers -** Thank you for giving me a chance. I did not set any expectations on *All I'll Ever Ask.* I just did my best and prayed the story would touch someone who read it. Words cannot express how thankful I am for the success of the debut novel for gdwoodsbooks.com. Thank you to everyone who downloaded a kindle copy, ordered a paperback, or purchased one at the Booksellers of Laurelwood. However, you meet the characters of the Greatest Love Series, I appreciate you for taking the time to read the story out of my imagination.

**Ms. Melissa Harrison** – Thank you for your editing services. I am grateful for every grammatical error you caught and for keeping me technically in line. I appreciate you taking me on and look forward to working with you in the future.

**Hubby** – Thank you for all the early mornings you were up with me as these characters' lives were unfolding. You never complained, you just awakened, wiped the sleep from your eyes, and helped birth these characters. These are our babies and we love them. I love you from the deepest place in my soul to the smile you bring across my lips. I would be lost without you.

**Mrs. LaShawn Vasser** –Thank you for taking time out of your busy schedule to read and offer me insight; *After Church* would not be possible without your encouragement.

**JB Logic Covers** – Thank you, the cover is perfect. I asked you for dark and spiritual and you delivered. Who knew I would have a mental battle over one little suggestion?

**Patrick, Debra, Tarsha, Daddy, Phyllis and Albertina, Dee-Dee, Joe Jr, and Barbara Ward** – Thank you for becoming book pushers. It means so much to me to have your support. Let's do it again.

**Pastor Gering** – Thank you for allowing me to adapt your sermon Baggage Sunday.

**Parents – To my parents Wade & Martha**, thank you for supporting my writing career. Daddy thanks for selling so many books. Mom thanks for challenging my word choice and giving me your opinion on every scene. To my Mother, Father, and Sister in Law, Carlene, Norbert & Angelica, I could not have married into a better family, thanks for allowing Sunday dinners to become strategy sessions.

**Nana Brenda and Papa Joe Bowen**, thanks for encouraging me and buying so many books for family and friends. Papa thank you for taking care of me when I was ill. **Aunt Lillie** your consistent love for me is an anchor in my life. I love you all!

**Phillip Woods** – Thank you for allowing me to use your illness for Nikki, and helping me write the scene. You are such a strong young man. I'm proud to be your mommy.

**Beta Readers – Jasmine Joyner, Mia Cobb Jackson, Kingston Westmoreland, Patrick E. Woods.** Thank you for your time and honest feedback.

**Nicole Vinson** -  bloomtheblog.com, Thank you for allowing me to adapt the boyfriend's prayer for Camille.

**Teety Blue** – Thank you for the soul searching instrumental for the book trailer. You are a talented young lady, I'm proud to be your big sister.

To the **Savior of my soul**, thank you for breathing this vision into me. May the words of my mouth and meditation of my heart, be pleasing and acceptable in thy sight. My Rock and Redeemer!

*Dedication:*

*This book is dedicated to the memory of my grandmother,*

*Momma Gladys Hightower.*

*You left us in March 2001 it feels like yesterday.*

*You are missed every day of our lives.*

*Previously in All I Ever Ask*
*Baggage Sunday*

The altar at Liberty Fellowship Church was decorated with luggage of all sizes and colors. Camille looked up as she walked down the aisle and saw the suitcases displayed on stage. There were more in front of the choir and orchestra. She wondered, "What on earth has Pastor Caine planned today?"

Entering the row where Mother Ellen sat, she was greeted with a warm smile. Standing to the right of Mother Ellen was Mrs. Carol. Camille went to greet her while repeating in her head, *it's nice to be nice…it's nice to be nice.* However, she did not have to worry about speaking to the unfriendly woman. Ms. Carol sat down and started rummaging through her purse to avoid speaking to Camille.

Mother Ellen compensated for Mrs. Carol's less than Christian attitude. She took Camille's purse and bible case. "Daughter that was some wedding you girls pulled off yesterday. It was beautiful. I can hardly wait to see what yours and Ben's will look like in a few months."

That brought out a genuine smile from Camille. She loved how Mother Ellen always referred to her as daughter.

Before Camille could respond, Ms. Carol looked up from her purse.

"Ellen, what are you talking about? I heard the cake fell apart. What is beautiful about that?" Mother Ellen's eyes bulged and nostrils flared. Camille would not have her going there with Ms. Carol.

"Mother Ellen you are so kind. I am happy Karen has what she deserves with Frankie and Nikki. They have both gone through so much. I pray they are satisfied with their day. I am certainly looking forward to planning our wedding, with your help of course. I am honored Ben believes I am the one for him."

"Well believe it daughter, because it is true and I believe it too. By the way, where is that son of mine?" Mother Ellen was turning and looking toward all the entrances for her son. Camille's eyes drifted up to the overhead monitor where the media team had the countdown clock displayed. It was twelve minutes until the service began. She had not spoken to Ben since he dropped her off last night.

"I am not sure where he is, let me text him. I am sure he is in the building somewhere." As she typed, her attention was drawn to Mrs. Carol who looked as if she had something to add to the "Where is Ben?" conversation.

"Maybe Ben would like to sit with just his two mothers today, me and Ellen. You have really inserted yourself everywhere in his life. There was a time, before you joined this church and stole him away that Ben would sit between us. Maybe he has come to his senses and this is a sign you need to back off!"

Mother Ellen turned and said, "Carol that is enough! Ben can sit wherever he chooses and he wants to sit near his fiancée. If you can't keep your responses to yourself, I suggest – you move!" Camille, frozen in her seat, sat facing forward unable to see how Mrs. Carol responded to the scolding. Her ears were burning from being caught off guard and insulted by Mrs. Carol's jab. How could this lady be so evil in the house of the Lord? Camille looked around the nearly full to capacity sanctuary and spotted Paige near the back. She grabbed her purse and bible. Mother Ellen tried to stop her and she paused. Camille gathered her emotions and addressed her with as much respect as possible.

"Mother Ellen please let me go. I will sit with Paige and Kevin, when Ben comes just tell him where I am." She kissed Mother Ellen on the cheek and made a mad dash to sit with her best friend. As she greeted Paige, she tried to check her embarrassment and frustration in the aisle.

The service was to begin in five minutes when Camille noticed Ben entering to sit by his mother. She could not believe it when she saw Mrs. Carol moving over and motioning with her hands for Ben to sit down in between them. Paige calling her name interrupted her eye stalking.

"Camille, why are you back here, and Ben is up there?"

"Um, Err… I just wanted to sit with my BFF."

"Why?"

"Because Paige, let's just enjoy the service. The praise and worship team is about to get started."

Ben closed his eyes, as he stood singing "Amazing Grace" along with the Praise and Worship Team. He was considering partnering with the music ministry. He needed to use the gift of voice the Lord blessed him with. He was late entering the service because his Sunday school class went over the time allotted for class. They were discussing the life of Apostle Paul and the time had escaped them. Had he known Camille would not sit in her normal seat, by him, he would have left class early. He thought when he texted her where he was she would have sat tight. Her absence was making it hard for him to focus on the worship in the auditorium. There was also something strange going on with his mom. She seemed to be in a bad mood. Not to mention, Mother Carol trying to make him sit in between them; he hated sitting in between them. He was a thirty-something year old man, for goodness sake. He suffered through months of that, after Lauren's death, and only because Mother Carol was grieving. However, enough was enough. The Lord had healed him and given him another chance at love. His mom and scripture taught him that Christians should bear one another's burdens but he would not be holding Mrs. Carol's hand any longer.

When Elder John completed the welcome and said to go greet someone, he ran to Camille with his I-Pad in hand. Experiencing the worship service and God's word with his lady next to his side was how Ben had started each week for the last several months. Today would be no different. He entered the row and grabbed Camille's hand. Ben shook it as if she was the queen of England and sang the greeting song of Liberty to her. "Good Morning Sister. The Jesus in me loves the Jesus in you. The Jesus in me loves the Jesus in you, you're easy, so easy, you're easy, easy to love." Camille blushed. What could a girl do after that, but smile and enjoy the remainder of the service.

Paige watched the two lovebirds as the choir sang. She could not wait to get to the bottom of this musical chair

act between Benjamin and Camille. However, for now she
had to key into the service. Kevin had given her notice that
she had to change. More than his notice, Paige knew she
needed to change. This was the best place for her to start.
The choir was singing "This Is Holy Ground". Paige had to
admit this choir could really sing.

No, it's the anointing, she thought. Paige smirked.
Listen to me already feeling a shift within my spirit. She
rose to her feet, pulled her hands together to her breast, and
closed her eyes as she let the lyrics break up the fallow
ground in her heart and mind.

*This is Holy ground,*

*we're standing on Holy ground*

*For the Lord is here*

*and where he is, is Holy*

*This is holy ground,*

*We're standing on Holy Ground*

*For the Lord is here*

*and where he is, is Holy*

*We are standing on Holy ground.*

*And I know that these are angels all around*

*Let us praise Jesus now*

*We are standing in Your presence, on Holy*

*ground.*

With each visit to Liberty, Kevin was drawn into this Protestant way of worship and lifestyle. It was vastly different from his Catholic upbringing, but he could feel the presence of the angels that the choir just finished singing about. He was also blown away by the luggage on display. Kevin was anxiously anticipating what Pastor Caine would lecture about using luggage. In his bulletin, there was a note card with a question, "What is your baggage?"

Kevin compared the service to a college course. He supposed that this was the best way to deliver instructions that could be applied by anyone who heard. According to Elder John, all the services were televised and streamed online, so there could actually be millions of people hearing the word of God. Kevin sat up in his seat as Pastor Caine came on the stage with luggage chained to his body. The lead pastor was about to fall face forward but he caught himself and began to deliver what Kevin, and most in attendance, considered a timely word. Pastor Caine delivered a message about "Traveling Light."

*"To do that in today's society is difficult because we are weighted down with baggage. There are 4 types of baggage: 1) Personal, 2) Work, 3) Church, 4) Other People's."*

Kevin was intrigued by this analogy. Pastor Caine was on the mark with him when it came to Personal and Work baggage.

*"As individuals, we try to be light and happy. We try to leave our unhappiness at the door. As the ushers escort us to our seats, we put on a smile trying to forget our failures, fears, and regrets but the personal baggage is stuck to us like glue. It is chained to us."*

Kevin could agree to that in his mind, heart, and soul, because his personal baggage was flowing over to his work baggage. It all was becoming too heavy, causing him both doubt and anxiety. As a public figure, he had to be transparent in all aspects of his life. Could he hold on to Paige and continue up the corporate ladder? Could he let go of the regret when perpetrators went free because of the negligence of his office, leaving victims hurting? He wanted to release these burdens but another issue was plaguing his heart. He always understood Peter was the rock that we should lean on for strength to be the Christian example. This is what he learned from the nuns. Jesus told Peter, "Upon this Rock I will build my church." Kevin shook that off. He assumed that was church baggage he needed to cast away. The more he attended the services and classes at Liberty; the more he believed that Jesus Christ himself was that rock.

As Kevin pondered those questions, Paige could do nothing but close her eyes as Pastor Caine continued the message that was nothing but the truth for her. Pastor Caine had one baggage for personal. Paige, if she was honest with herself, had dozens of personal baggage chained to her. As Pastor Caine explained how personal baggage came to be, he was telling the story of her life. Her baggage began before she could remember. Her mother was addicted to drugs, causing her to care for herself as a toddler. That began her need for self–preservation, by any means necessary, to take root. Add to that every family hurt, including being sexually violated, verbally abused and continually neglected—Paige was left chained and bound. Tears began to stream as she received Pastor Caine's words of redemption.

He explained 1 Peter 5:7. *"Cast all your anxiety on him because he cares for you."* Paige repeated that last phrase silently to herself. "He cares for me." She had a heavenly father that cared for her and who wanted her baggage. Instantly her mind went to Kevin who wanted her to release the anger, venom, and vicious self-protection mask. Now, she knew the Savior above wanted the same thing for her. Paige looked in the bulletin and grabbed the blank note card that read, "What's your baggage?" She began to write down every heavy burden that was chained to her.

Camille was already writing down her baggage. She was weighed down with personal issues. Fear of telling Karen that they were possibly sisters, and the disappointment that her father was not the superman she believed he was all of her life. Her disappointment was leading her to doubt if Benjamin was her Adam or like her dad, too good to be true. Her work baggage was full of imbalance and the need to work long hours to prevent her fear of failure. Just this morning Camille strapped on baggage for church hurt. Mrs. Carol gifted that piece of luggage with her ugly remarks and mean spirit. Nevertheless, she was determined to cast all these cares on the Master. According to Pastor Caine and Peter, He wanted her burdens and anxiety.

Benjamin's chained baggage was that he held other people's baggage. Pastor Caine's message was divinely inspired. Benjamin received from it that he could help carry Mrs. Carol's burden of grief by praying for her, giving her a listening ear, helping her enroll in counseling, and showing her love. However, he could not let her refusal to heal from grief become his baggage. The light bulb went off for Ben. If he continued to carry Lauren's mother's grief, he would lose his future. Ben wrote a one-liner on his baggage card, *other peoples.*

In twenty-two minutes, Pastor Caine delivered a message of deliverance. As he ministered, he started to unlock and remove the chained luggage on his person. He explained Hebrews 12:1, *"Therefore, since we are surrounded by such a great cloud of witnesses, let us throw off everything that hinders and the sin that so easily entangles. And let us run with perseverance the race marked out for us."*

Pastor Cain finished the sermon asking a key question.

*"Have you entered the race with Christ? If you are not in the race, you must accept Jesus as your personal savior. If you are in the race, you must prepare yourself to finish the race well. A runner when racing dresses light so they may run a diligent race. We as Christians cannot run diligently if we are loaded with baggage. Therefore, we must cast and throw down the weights of: not forgiving others, anxiety, and doubt. We must do away with sins; doing things, we know are wrong. We must look to Jesus for our help. It is not always easy to do this. Liberty Church is here to help you. We offer free counseling for*

*individuals, couples, family, and grief counseling by licensed therapists.*"

Pastor Caine extended his hands toward the congregation. *"The praise and worship team is coming to minister to our hearts through song. Please take your notecards and list the baggage you want to release today. Come throw it on the altar and leave it there. The elders are here to pray with you and the spirit of Christ is here to heal you.*"

The praise and worship ministry began to sing Tasha Cobb's version of "Break Every Chain". The aisles of the sanctuary were filled with people eager to release their baggage and lay aside their weights and sin. Kevin, Paige, Camille, and Benjamin were among those people.

Not one of them would ever be the same again.

## *Chapter 1*
### *Reflections*

It was five o'clock in the morning, as Karen walked barefoot along the shoreline of the Atlantic Ocean. She was taking in the picturesque scenery. It was the first morning of her honeymoon with Frankie, and their three-year-old daughter, Nikki. Frankie and Nikki were asleep in their condominium. The thought of being someone's wife made Karen smile and shake her head in disbelief. She thought about the charming ceremony and reception she had yesterday. Although, something did not sit right with her about her cake collapsing; nevertheless, she and her friends were able to pull together a fabulous day in just two weeks. It was a long and exhausting day. The night was made even longer as she and her family caught the last flight from Memphis, Tennessee to Hilton Head, South Carolina. They were staying at the Disney Resort on the island. She and Frankie had chosen to bring Nikki on their honeymoon, because she was the catalyst that allowed their love to be possible.

It was after midnight when they arrived and Karen was exhausted. However, she was up at 4:30 a.m. too excited to sleep. She was full of nervous energy from the events of the past twenty-four hours. She didn't want to wake her husband and daughter, she decided to go for a walk to think. As she walked down the beach, she was in awe of how life could change so quickly.

Karen inhaled fresh air from the breeze that came off the ocean's waves. She stopped to admire the exquisite site of the slow sunrise, while the cool waves forcefully came up to her ankles. How wonderful that God spoke this into existence. It was marvelous and she gave thanks to the Creator of All, for this beautiful day that He had made.

Karen began to walk again, smiling at the other early risers along the way. Some were walking, while others were riding bikes. She could not wait to experience this magnificent island and the rich traditions it held with Frankie and Nikki.

Karen began to recall the countless moments that she experienced trauma and disappointment in her life. Knowing where she came from simply made her present situation unbelievable. Karen had kept her past buried within herself, only telling Camille vaguely about her mother's death. And how she lived on her own, as a teenager. Her past life was a deck of cards she preferred to hold close to her chest. She rationalized that it did not matter where she had come from, only where she was now, and where she would be in the future.

However, sometimes like now, when all was right in the world, she had to look back at all she had escaped. She had committed some unimaginable deeds to get where she was. She had been through so much, starting with losing her mother to murder as a child—a murder that had eventually been classified as a cold case. Karen was then awarded by the state of Tennessee; to an aunt she had only met a couple of times. Aunt Esther, who lived in Little Rock, Arkansas, had always seemed okay the couple of times Karen met her; but living with her proved differently. Aunt Esther treated Karen awful. Aunt Esther used her for housekeeping, babysitting, and entertainment needs. If Karen didn't do a task to Aunt Esther's satisfaction she was physically beaten. Surviving the pain of her adolescent years and not being consumed by it all, was because of the Lord's mercy. That thought reminded Karen of one of her favorite gospel songs by Eddie James. She pulled out her mobile and pulled up the music app. She scrolled down to her encouragement playlist, that her best friend and boss Camille had made for her, and selected "Great is thy Faithfulness." Karen listened to the lyrics that could have been written exclusively for her. The song, spoke of looking back over one's past and seeing that the Lord has always been there, blessing and protecting them. It referenced Lamentations 3:22-24: "It is of the LORD's mercies that we are not consumed, because his compassions fail not. They are new every morning: great is thy faithfulness."

Karen allowed her mind to go back to the horrors she endured day after day with Aunt Esther, who saw her as nothing more than a means to an end. One way was the monthly government check she received. Aunt Esther rarely purchased Karen anything outside of the two meals she ate daily and the roof over her head. In addition to the check, there was the money that came from the men that Aunt Esther would force Karen to be with. Karen endured sexual abuse for years until she couldn't take it any longer. At the age of sixteen, she ran away from what should have been a home but was nothing more than a brothel. She lived as a ragamuffin on the streets and soon joined a gang called The Crew. The gang members were her family. She took care of them and they did the same for her.

Taking care of The Crew was not as straightforward as Aunt Esther's demands; she committed crimes in the name of the "family" against others. She had gone from bad to worse. She did not enjoy the illegal and dark parts of gang life, but what could she do? The Crew members protected her from the worst elements of the street life. By the time she was eighteen, she was in love with her best friend Mario Clemmons, another run-a-way who was making his way up in rank with The Crew.

Karen grimaced. As a mature adult with a daughter, she realized what a risk she had taken by joining The Crew. She would never want that for Nikki and would do everything possible to keep her from making the same mistakes. The fact that she joined a gang to have some semblance of family, she knew was sad. Back then, she didn't know any better and it was her only way to survive. The only person that loved her was dead, and if she had continued to live with Aunt Esther, she would have become a murderer. Her anger, hatred, and resentment ran that deep for Aunt Esther. Karen was never able to have any type of closure with her aunt. She was contacted by the State of Arkansas several years ago to claim Aunt Esther's body. She had died of a stroke. Karen went back and claimed the body, paid to have it cremated, and sold the house. She donated the proceeds of the sale to a local charity for homeless teens. Remembering herself as a teen, she thought she needed The Crew. They made her feel wanted; the first time since her mother's death she belonged to someone other than herself.

Little did she know when she joined that she did indeed belong to The Crew, and there was only one way out of their *"family."* She found out how on a fateful night that changed her life forever. The night she was robbed of her soul and whipped within an inch of her life.

After spending years in The Crew doing things she would take to her grave, it was a miracle she was never arrested for her crimes. Mario was the reason for that. He always made sure that no evidence pointed in her direction. She wanted out of the life before that changed and she was locked behind bars like so many of her CREW family. She convinced herself she would be okay with conveying that to Leroy, her block captain. Karen thought she had a great reason for them to let her go; she was twenty-two years old now and pregnant. She wanted to enroll in Junior College. When Mario started making enough money to pay their bills, she went to night school, studied for the test, and earned her GED. She desperately wanted her baby and to have a gang-free life.

She did not tell Mario about her plan. She felt she could handle the backlash from him after it was over. She knew Mario had her back and would take care of her, he always had. She had been so wrong. Karen had been naïve to think that she could just say, "Hey I have decided to be a normal citizen, I plan to go to college, and have my baby. Thanks for allowing me to kick it with you for the past six years and for making sure, I survived the streets as a runaway. Deuces!"

Karen's entire being still quaked when she recalled the way Leroy's eyes changed from a light brown to nearly black, and his hand lifted and came down on her face with a resounding slap. Karen's ears began to ring. Blood escaped from her mouth and gushed from her nose. Leroy shouted his spittle landing on the side of her burning face.

"There is only one way out this mf'er and that is with a life! It can be yours, that seed in your belly, or both, doesn't matter to me shorty, but that is how you resign from The Crew!"

In a flash the beating resumed, and left her with a detached retina in one eye (that was currently held together by a surgical buckle), a broken arm, and emotional scars that remained to this day.

After Leroy was satisfied that he had beaten Karen close enough to death he called Mario. Leroy informed him that a runner had dropped Karen off at the Emergency Room. After Mario eyeballed the injuries Leroy had inflicted on his love, he was in a frenzy. He comforted Karen, and assured her of his love. He promised her she would have their baby, a beautiful little girl. He made a vow to her that everything would be ok. When Karen drifted off to sleep that night, Mario went to confront Leroy. However, Mario did not receive an explanation for his concerns, nor did he receive a beat down like Karen. Leroy quietly took out his gun and shot Mario in between the eyes, while members of The Crew watched. Mario's body was disposed of and Karen never got a chance to say goodbye.

Karen was in the hospital when she received the news and suffered a miscarriage, their little girl would never be. She was left feeling guilt for Mario and their unborn child's death. She carried the guilt, pain, and shame silently. That night haunted Karen in her dreams incessantly.

To ensure she never forgot all she had lost, she celebrated annually the anniversary of the night she lost it all. It was her very own holiday of lamentations and regrets. On that death day—D-Day— she would drink herself into a stupor. She would drink until she had lost all feeling emotionally and was physically numb. She felt she deserved to be miserable; everything that happened that night was her fault. Therefore, each year on D-Day she would lose herself in alcohol and some type of drug. She would grieve for what and who she lost due to her poor choices.

It was on one of those nights, years later that Frankie approached her at the bar in Huey's Restaurant on Madison, Avenue in Memphis, Tennessee. She had been sitting there for three hours ordering drink after drink. It had only taken Frankie asking once for her to agree to a hook up with him at a local hotel. Karen went with the stranger whose last name she did not know, because she needed to free herself from the guilt. She went and when Frankie sat down at the table in their shabby room, he readied lines of cocaine. He passed her the rolled up dollar, she took it, and snorted the blow.

Karen wiped the tears from her face. Others on the beach were starting to stare at her crying. The lyrics to her song, which was on auto-repeat, rang true to her core. *It was because of the Lord's mercy that she was not consumed.*

Mario's death was enough for the high-ranking officers of The Crew to let her go. When she was released from the hospital, she scurried back to Memphis with the money from her joint bank account with Mario. It was enough for her to rent a one-bedroom apartment—paying eighteen months in advance, buy furniture, and food.

Karen began to work as a waitress at a strip club and eventually became an exotic dancer. She stayed clear of any drugs and alcohol, using her money to pay for tuition at the community college she attended. She started off doing only lap dances, which ended on the first year anniversary of Mario's death. That night she got drunk and went home with a stranger, experimented with ecstasy, and had sex until the early morning. The next day she re-grouped and lived her life as if nothing happened; she continued to do the same thing every year after.

Karen kept her dark secret. She could not break the habit no matter how her life changed for the better. She met Camille James when she was hired as an intern at I.T.S, and was elated to find out Ms. James was the owner. Camille was impressive, with beauty, brains, and a good heart. The two of them developed a friendship immediately and she could not have asked for a better boss or friend. Karen was hired full time as Camille's Executive Assistant upon obtaining her Associates Degree in Business. I.T.S had an awesome benefits package, with health insurance, vacation, sick days, and tuition reimbursement. Camille encouraged her to go back for her Bachelor's Degree. Then she met Paige Richards, a totally hotheaded diva, who made Karen want to call on her street days and beat some sense into her. She could not do that because Paige came with Camille's package. However, over the years the three of them had become sisters and had one another's back.

Despite all the good things in her life, it was finding out that she was pregnant that stopped D-Day from recurring. Karen would never regret Nikki. She had saved her. Now she had Frankie, and although she abhorred the precarious behavior she chose to numb her guilt and pain, she knew she was blessed. She knew it could have turned out tragically. But God! What was the likelihood that she would have a chance reunion with Frankie? When Camille was in the hospital, recovering from being hit by a drunken driver, she and Nikki had needed a ride home. Paige and Kevin agreed to take her, only Kevin needed to stop by his office. They walked into the Assistant District Attorney's lobby and the mail courier was engaged in a conversation with members of Kevin's staff.

"Hey, Frankie. I'd like to introduce you to my girlfriend Paige." Frankie smiled as he directed his attention to Paige and Kevin.

"Hi Paige, it's good to meet you." He shook hands with her and then Kevin.

When Kevin turned to introduce Karen and Nikki, they were both frozen in a daze of disbelief. Frankie looked from her to Nikki and he knew immediately. Paige and Kevin looked at Frankie and Karen, and back to each other.

"I guess you've met Karen?" Kevin asked.

The question broke the spell that Frankie and Karen had been under. After briefly explaining to Kevin and Paige how they had met, they all quietly understood who Frankie was to Nikki. She resembled him, having his eye color, chin, and her little crooked smile matched his. Nikki held out her hand to shake his.

"Hi, I am Nikki Locke. What's your name?" Frankie, with tears in his eyes, gave her a handshake and grabbed her up in a hug. Once his emotions were under control, they exchanged contact information and he reluctantly continued his delivery route.

Frankie came to her apartment that same night and they talked for hours and had been together since. Now they were married. If someone had told her a year ago that Frankie would find them and marry her, no less, she wouldn't have believed them.

She had a lingering thought in the back of her mind that God allowed Mario's promise to her to come true, everything was ok. Karen smiled again feeling the impact of the lyrics streaming through her earbuds. She entered into the luxury condo where her family was sleeping with a heart full of gratitude. She was singing, "I can never repay You Lord for what You done for me. How You loosed my shackles and you set me free. How You made a way out of no way, turned my darkness into day."

*Chapter 2*

*A Balm*


*2 Weeks Later*

"Camille, I can't thank you and Ben enough for allowing us to store these gifts here." Karen and Frankie were at Benjamin's house to open up the *hundreds* of wedding gifts they received. She and Camille were now stacking the duplicates and questionable gifts in Benjamin's basement. Camille had made the evening a family night. Dawn, Autumn, Tabitha, and Kierra were over for the gift-unwrapping, but Paige and Kevin could not attend. Paige was in her weekly counseling session and Kevin had taken a trip to Atlanta to visit his parents.

"Well, we will both have to thank Benjamin, it's his house."

"It will be your home in a couple of months. I noticed you have already started making décor changes."

"I had to— this place was a serious bachelor's pad. I couldn't continue to visit and look at all the lion décor he had around here and the black and brown in every room was not working. The first thing I threw out was that picture of the black man holding the world on his shoulders. No one has asked a black man or any man for that matter, to hold the world up with his bare hands. Then it was like The Lion King in here, at any moment, I felt Simba and Nyla would come running through the room, singing "I Just Can't Wait to be King." They both fell into fits of laughter. The basement door opened, and they looked toward it to see who was coming. Tabitha, Ben's cousin who was raised with him after her parents were killed in a car crash, along with Dawn were coming down with more gifts to store. Camille went to assist Tabitha, and Karen grabbed the boxes out of Dawn's hands.

"Tabitha, thank you so much for helping us." Camille said, as she took a box from her. There was an image on the box of an ugly, white, ceramic figurine. Camille scrunched up her nose at the gift. She thought, *would it be rude to only ask for gift cards at my reception? Yeah, that would be rude.* She would talk to Benjamin about asking their wedding attendees to donate to a charity on their behalf, maybe a breast cancer foundation. Or one of the sickle cell anemia foundations or juvenile diabetes, one of those in lieu of gifts. If she was ever in need of a crockpot, skillet, coffee pot, teakettle, picture frame, or books about marriage, she could just come downstairs.

Karen had received too many of them. Tabitha, calling her name, interrupted her wedding planning thoughts.

"Camille, don't be silly. You and Karen would be here all night storing these gifts. The guys are up there playing pool, like they don't see us hauling these boxes down these stairs." Tabitha set the boxes down and took a seat on a trunk to catch her breath.

Dawn chimed in. "I'm happy to bring these gifts down. I would rather do manual labor than watch Frozen again. I love my little sister, but I can't take one more viewing of that movie." They all laughed. "I can't believe Nikki can watch that movie non-stop. It's to the point where I'm about to break baby girl's heart and tell her we will never be able to build a snowman. We live in Memphis we get ice, not snow." Everyone in the basement was full of laughter, but Dawn was serious. Autumn had the patience for the movie watching and coloring. She would leave that to her and just take the little diva shopping.

Karen was still laughing as she looked around the basement. Their gifts had taken up quite a bit of space. Dawn and Tabitha had gone back up and were now coming down with another handful.

"I didn't expect to receive so many gifts, although some I have no idea why anyone would purchase. Nonetheless, I am grateful that we were thought of, and people wanted to celebrate our union. I was amazed when I looked at the registry book and saw close to three hundred people attended. I have been alone for so long, just me, then Camille came into my life as a boss, and quickly became my best friend. I have never had a friend like you before." Karen looked directly at Camille as she made the declaration. "Then Nikki, who was a shock but a wonderful blessing. Now, I stand here with a husband, family, and friends, it is all overwhelming." Karen jerked tears from all the ladies with her emotional speech. Dawn went to hug her stepmother.

"Karen, you are such a beautiful person. I'm happy dad has you in his life." Karen hugged Dawn back as the tears fell from her eyes, into Dawn's long wavy auburn hair. Karen had quickly developed a close relationship with both of Frankie's daughters. Camille and Tabitha looked at the stepmother and daughter with their own tears flowing.

Camille's heart started to race. Karen had more family under this roof then she knew, as Camille herself was holding hostage the secret of Karen's paternity. She knew she needed to tell Karen, but she was afraid of her reaction to the news. Benjamin had scolded her earlier for procrastinating. He insisted she tell Karen the truth as soon as possible. He thought tonight would've been the perfect opportunity, and was furious with her when she invited more guests to attend.  He told her she invited the others as a diversion to avoid telling Karen the truth. Camille did not think Benjamin understood what she could lose if Karen didn't take the news well. Karen's friendship was important to her; she only had a few people in this world she could not imagine life without.  Karen was on that list. What would happen to their friendship? Would she quit I.T.S? Would she keep Nikki away from her?  Benjamin had told her if she really loved Karen and valued their friendship she would tell her sooner rather than later. Camille told him she was afraid. Ben had the audacity to say to her, "There is no fear in love. But perfect love drives out fear." Camille could not believe he threw a scripture at her, and then he left her alone in the kitchen while she was preparing their dinner. What she really wanted to know was who argues quoting scriptures? Camille was snapped out of her thoughts as Karen called her name.

"Camille."

"I'm sorry, I drifted off."

"Is it okay, if Dawn and Autumn come over to get the things they need for their new apartment?"

"Sure, just let me know when." Camille turned to speak to Dawn. "I heard you and Autumn transferred to the local university."

"Yes, we wanted to be near our family, especially since our…umm… our mother, she is… she is not." Karen saved Dawn the trouble of finishing her thoughts.

"Yes, Dawn and Autumn are so thoughtful, their mother is not handling Frankie marrying me well. I think it is wonderful that they care so deeply for their mother to move home to help her adjust to our blended family. I can only hope that Nikki, will have such dedication to me when she is older." Dawn was grateful for the save. She took Karen's hand while speaking to the group.

"Karen, we did not move back home only to keep an eye on mom. We love you and Nikki as well. We want to spend as much time with our family as possible. I'm proud of dad and happy he has this new beginning." Karen embraced Dawn. The night was turning into nothing but girl mush.

The mush turned to hysteria, as Benjamin ran down the stairs, screaming. "Cam, Karen, come up stairs, something is wrong with Nikki!"

Karen jumped up and pushed passed Benjamin as she made her way up the basement stairs. When she entered the den, where Frankie held Nikki, Autumn was trying to force liquid anti-histamine down Nikki's throat, but failing. She froze. The sight of her baby's limp body dangling in Frankie's arms stopped time for Karen. Nikki's eyes were open but she could not see her pupils, her face was swollen, and there were hives on every visible part of her little body. Suddenly, Karen felt her limbs become free from paralysis. She grabbed Nikki out of Frankie's arms, checked her mouth and saw her tongue was swelling. Before she could react, she heard the sirens of the ambulance. "Great," she thought, "someone called 9-1-1!"

It seemed like hours but it was only minutes. The paramedics gave Nikki an antihistamine injection that stopped the swelling. The innumerable amount of hives that formed on Nikki's small body was frightening but they were disappearing. The paramedics asked, "Who are the parents of the child?"

Karen spoke up. "I am her mother." She pointed in Frankie's direction. "This is her father."

"Has your daughter experienced a histamine attack of this nature before?"

"No, not like this. We were recently in Hilton Head, South Carolina, and she got hives. I took her to the doctor when we got back. The doctor told me to give her over the counter antihistamine. She said it may have been the freshness of the seafood."

"Ok, well we think you should make an appointment with an allergist as soon as possible. A few more minutes and Nikki could have been in a calamitous situation."

"Ok, we will." Karen said, while holding Nikki so tightly, Frankie thought she would suffocate her.

"Yes thank you all, for coming out so quickly. We will be sure to make an appointment tomorrow. Are you sure she doesn't need to go to the Emergency room?" Frankie asked the paramedics as he walked them out.

"Only if she appears to have another histamine attack. That should not be the case though; we have given her an ample dose of anti-histamine."

"Ok, thank you again."

"Have a nice evening sir."

Frankie closed and locked the front door. He headed back to the den where everyone was doting over a now responsive Nikki. He was grateful to see his baby girl doing better. He thought he was going to have a heart attack when

Kierra ran in the game room screaming, "Nikki is not breathing." He said a prayer of thanks for Jesus being a healer and balm tonight. They would have to get Nikki into a specialist's office first thing tomorrow morning.

***

The tension was palpable as the kitchen staff was serving the Michelson's family. Kevin couldn't remember eating a meal his mother, Julia, had made in his life. His chest was tight from the anticipation of the pending conversation and he had no appetite whatsoever. He was ready to get this over with. He had driven six-hours into town to speak with his parents about Paige.

It had been three weeks since he and Paige decided to reconcile. Paige was at her second counseling session tonight, to start working on her demons as she termed it. Kevin was hopeful, that she would find the resolve or deliverance she needed to lose her Raige persona.

He was here tonight to address his parents or more accurately, his mother's concerns regarding Paige. However, his mother being the epitome of the classical southern lady insisted they have a proper family dinner first. She also made it clear that the dialogue could not begin until the staff was out of hearing range. Kevin was always baffled how his mother could pick certain etiquettes to follow, while neglecting others.  It was entertaining and frustrating to watch a woman, who would literally spit on another human being, forbid any conversations regarding family issues in front of the help. What made her imposed rule more ridiculous was that, *the help* had worked for the family for decades.

Kevin thanked Mrs. Louise for serving him the Cornish hen, green beans, and scalloped potatoes. If truth be told, Mrs. Louise is the one he should call mother. Growing up, her face was the first one he saw when he woke each morning for school. She picked him up from his afterschool activities, made sure his homework was complete, and cooked his dinner.  His own mother was always busy being the wife of a successful attorney then judge. That was neither here nor there now. He came here with a purpose and that was to set the record straight with his mother concerning his affairs with Paige.

Surprisingly, his father spoke first, which never happened. All of Kevin's life, his father let his other half control the dinner conversations and everything else at the Michelson's manor.

"Son, how is everything going at the D.A.'s office?"

"It's been busy and trying dad, but I'm hanging in there."

"Any important cases? I try to check on you as much as possible. However, my own docket has been full the last month or so."

"Nothing major since we got the conviction and sentencing on the massacre that happened on Phoenix Street. That case almost took the life out of me. Hopefully and prayerfully I won't have to prosecute anything that atrocious again."

"Hopefully not. I've never had to experience a defendant as wicked as that one. But you proved why you are next in line to be the District Attorney."

"Kevin did not need that appalling case to prove his worth." Mrs. Michelson interrupted, deciding to drop her vow of silence. "He is the best attorney that tacky city could ever dream of having to protect them." Before Kevin could thank his mother for the backhanded compliment, she went on. "Speaking of tacky, I am so happy you ended that terrible relationship with Paige. Now you can find a more appropriate companion."

"And it begins," Kevin thought. He glanced at his father but as usual, he did not take his eyes off the Cornish hen. Why couldn't he be Judge Michelson under his own roof? Instead, he allowed his wife and son to argue their cases without a mediator.

"Mother, I know I told you a few weeks ago that Paige and I ended things. That was temporary. We are back together now and I will be asking her to marry me soon. My reason for coming is to make you and dad aware of my decision. I also need to ask you to call a truce with Paige."

"Steven Roger Michelson, please tell me you didn't hear your son say he was considering marrying that—hussy."

"Mother, there is no need for dad to answer that question. I said, I will be asking Paige to marry me. I am not considering it; it is a promise that I will deliver."

"Kevin Anthony Michelson, you do recall that she attacked me? I did not press charges because you said that was the end of your sordid affair with that wretched girl. You can't, and won't, be giving common trash our name. I simply won't have it."

"Mother, how do you suppose you will stop me?"

"I will press charges against her."

"I will get her the best attorney."

"She will never be welcome here, in my home."

"If that is the way you want it mother, fine! Paige won't come to your home again and neither will I!" Kevin used the cloth napkin to wipe his hands and mouth. He rose from the table to retrieve his coat. He was done with this conversation and visit. Julia stood when she realized he was leaving and scurried behind him.

"Kevin, what are you saying? Are you choosing her over your own mother and father?"

"Mother, you are choosing your prejudice over me. Dad has never expressed any dislike regarding Paige that is all you. You speak as if you had no contribution in your fight with Paige. She told me how you degraded her deceased mother. For heaven's sake mom, you spat on her."

"Yes, I did. She called me a fake, female dog, only she used the B word."

"Mother, you provoked her. You don't know Paige's story because you have never given her a chance. I am telling you now; I will honor your wishes by staying away if Paige is not welcomed here. However, *I. Will. Marry. Her.* I am done discussing it. I was hoping you were willing to work it out with Paige, for me. Clearly you are not, so I know where I stand." Kevin already had his jacket on and was heading to leave.

Mrs. Louise was passing through the foyer; she had a look of remorse on her face, as if she could feel his pain. Kevin hurried to her and hugged her whispering in her ear. "I will call you soon."

She gave him a motherly kiss on the cheek and said, "Be careful and I couldn't be more proud of you, son."

Kevin looked over his shoulder to his father. "Dad I'll check on you when Paige and I are in town. I will call your office to schedule a time for us to see you." Kevin did not wait for a response; he knew his father would not utter one word that would upset his wife. As he opened the front door, his mother rushed behind him calling out his name. He stopped and turned, hoping against hope she had a change of heart.

"Kevin, you mark my words, hooking up with that vile girl will be the worst mistake ever. Nothing good can come from her. Nothing!" Kevin could not believe his mother's words. What was wrong with her?

"Mother, I have heard your warning, you need to heed mine! Don't. Mess. With. Paige. If you do, the only thing vile will be coming from me to you. Have a nice life mother!"

Kevin stormed out, slamming the door so hard the windows rattled. He got into his car, secured his seat belt, and slammed the car's door shut with so much force the driver's window shattered. He looked at the fallen glass in his lap, let out a frustrated groan, and wept in the circular driveway in front of his childhood home.

\*\*\*

"Paige, let's go over your assignment from last week. You were to make a list of your top five strengths and three areas you wanted to improve on your character. Do you have those?" Dr. Whitney Ann Kimball, who preferred to be called Dr. Whitney, was a beautiful forty-something year old woman. Paige admired how she always looked so put together. She wore a short bob with bangs; her hair was a strawberry blonde that went perfectly with her light caramel skin.

As she took out her portfolio, Paige wondered why the doctor had to give that long definition. It was redundant, but she went along with it. She opened the prongs and gave Dr. Whitney a copy of the list that contained her strengths, and weaknesses. She anxiously waited for Dr. Whitney to speak as she looked over her list.

After a couple of minutes, Dr. Whitney spoke. "Let's start with your strengths. You have listed first that you are a Survivor. Explain to me why this is the first strength you chose."

Paige took a moment to collect her thoughts. Counseling was difficult. It was you, the doctor, and your personal truths. As simple as it sounded, it was the opposite. Opening yourself up to someone else was hard. After a pregnant pause, Paige began.

"I chose being a survivor first, because that is who and what I am before anything else. Before I could write my own name, I had survived things most adults will never experience. When I was twelve years old, I read the police report on the incident of my mother being found dead, and me being with her. A sentence stuck out to me then and has been with me since. It said, 'There was a minor female on the scene who survived being alone with her mother's corpse.' That was the day I started calling myself a survivor. Long before Destiny's Child and the reality show were in existence, I was a survivor." Paige stopped speaking. She was choking up and the tears were falling freely. Dr. Whitney offered her tissues. Paige accepted them and began to blow her nose. Dr. Whitney coached her on breathing in and out so she could collect herself and avoid an anxiety attack. When Dr. Whitney was sure Paige was okay, she began again.

"Paige, how does that make you feel?"

"How does what make me feel?" Did she not just hear me say I felt like a survivor? Paige thought. There was no way she would be repeating herself.

"How does being termed, a survivor in the report, make you feel?"

"It makes me feel like all I was given to begin my life was a dead corpse of a mother for a foundation. It makes me feel like, every breath I have taken or will take, I have had to fight for. And in order for me to continue to breathe I have to fight anything or anyone that gets in my way."

Dr. Whitney nodded, signaling she accepted Paige's response. She then looked to Paige's response sheet and addressed her. "Is it safe to say, that has influenced your first item for improvement which is anger?"

"I don't know doctor, could be."

"Paige, I need you to answer all questions with thought. Let's try not to answer questions with I don't know. Is that agreeable?"

"I will try. But I don't know. That is why I am here, Doctor." Paige blew her nose in the Kleenex. "This is so hard; I don't know if my being neglected by my junkie mother caused my anger issues. Could be? I. Don't. Know. Maybe it's the fact that I don't have one memory of her. I've seen her in pictures when she was younger, she was beautiful. Maybe I am angry because I was not enough for her to stay off drugs. It could be that the people she left me with did not give a rat's ass about me."

Paige inhaled. She had used profanity, something she had sworn off weeks ago, but kept failing to hold true to the commitment. She was failing at this letting go of baggage bull. It was hard. It was safer behind the brick walls she had erected early in life. Behind her brick, emotional walls, no one could touch her. If they tried, she would come down on them and they would regret it. No! No! If she wanted to be free, she had to push forward. She could not tell Ms. Pretty Doctor to kiss her behind and leave. Her flesh wanted out, her walls wanted to remain erect, Raige, her protector, did not want to die. She wanted to tell Dr. Whitney that she was full of it and she would not be attending again. What was wrong with being angry and having walls? She didn't start anything, she only finished it, and last she checked that was called self-defense.

Dr. Whitney could see Paige's internal battle. She silently prayed that the Holy Spirit would enter the room and bring peace to Paige's troubled mind and soul. She spoke life into Paige while holding a trembling Paige's hands. After several long minutes, Paige shook away those wayward thoughts that were caused by fear.

"Dr. Whitney, I am sorry for using profanity. I have to stop cussing."

"Paige, it takes time to stop some habits, especially when that habit has been a form of self-protection for you. I have heard worse words. I also hear you may hold some resentment for your mother being addicted to drugs, which ultimately caused her demise. Do you agree with that?"

"Yes." Paige was nodding her head emphatically. "Yes, I do feel like my mother killing herself with drugs was the beginning of my anger issues."

"Why do you feel that way?"

"Because I am angry with her. I am angry that I wasn't worth staying clean for. I am angry because I wasn't worth her living for. I am angry she left me to take care of myself, and I have been doing it all my life the best way I knew how. By surviving, I now have wonderful friends and a man that loves me and I am near losing it all. Because my survival tactics WERE ALL WRONG!" Paige's voice cracked and the dam to her buried insecurities had broken at last. Dr. Whitney saw the levee break and squeezed Paige's hand as the words flowed from her soul.

"I am so angry with her because although she abandoned me by death, leaving me nothing— not even my father's name—in my heart, I love her so much. I will not tolerate any one speaking ill of her, I feel like I have to protect a memory of a ghost that haunts me.  Her death haunts me, because I wonder if she had lived, would I have these flaws, could I love without boundaries? Would I have all of this personal baggage Pastor Caine spoke about a couple of weeks ago? If she had cared enough about me and kicked that drug habit, would I be the person on the inside that I portray on the outside? I'm so messed up Dr. Whitney. I'm lost and the more I think about my life, the worse I feel, and then the angrier I become." Paige buried her face in the Kleenex that covered the palm of her hands. Dr. Whitney again gave her time. She moved to the flanking chair across from Paige and pulled her hands away from her face to get her attention.  Paige looked up into Dr. Whitney's compassionate face and tried to stop crying. Her cries slowly turned into hiccups. Dr. Whitney proceeded as the session was nearing its end.

"Paige, I know it may seem hard right now to understand the progress you have made in these two sessions. You have revealed a critical trigger for your anger and self-protection defenses. Now, what I want you to understand is you are not alone. We as Christians have a savior who is our healer. This sense of abandonment you feel, the lack of self-worth by your mother choosing drugs over your wellbeing, has made you independent and fierce. However, as the song goes, you can let Jesus take the wheel now.  Let Jesus be your balm, the healer of your broken heart." Dr. Whitney stood and went behind her desk and retrieved a tablet. "There are some points I want you to write down and meditate on this week. As well as some scriptures I want you to study and pray about implementing into your thoughts and reactions to situations.

Paige took out her portfolio and opened the section that contained her legal pad. Her tears had ceased and her breathing had finally returned to normal. She looked to Dr. Whitney, signaling she was ready for her to begin.

"One, it is okay to mourn over what you have lost. Paige, you lost the chance to have memories with your mother, a home with a mother and father. It's ok to be saddened by that. This week, write a list of other things this caused you to lose and grieve over them.

"Two, get back on track after you mourn what was lost. Get back on track by looking at all the positives in your life and future. Don't let this loss do, to your life, what the drugs did to your mother's. Recover and walk triumphantly over the hurt and the losses.

"Three, press on. Don't give in when the enemy tries to pull you back into the trap of grief or anger. Find a calming, encouraging scripture this week that lets you know you are an overcomer.

"Four, forgive so you may be forgiven. Forgive the people who come against you in words or deeds. Forgive people who come against your loved ones. Allow the Lord to fight your battles. Forgive your mother for not being strong enough to do what you are strengthened by Christ to do through him.

"These points are important for you to practice, so that you receive. Know that Jesus is with you and he is our healer, he is our present day Balm in Gilead. Let's pray as we have come to the close of our session today."

Paige bowed her head with Dr. Whitney and asked the Lord to help her accept him as her balm for emotional healing. After the prayer, Dr. Whitney gave her a booklet entitled "Calming Scriptures for Anger." She asked Paige to study them as her homework, and next week come prepared to share how it helped her release anger. Paige hugged Dr. Whitney, and complimented her on her Red-

Bottom shoes and all black designer pantsuit. Dr. Whitney was truly a Diva in the Lord. She responded with a humble "Thank you" and told Paige to be blessed.

Paige had to stop and confirm her appointment with the receptionist, Tamala Sykes, who was another Diva in the Lord. She was a beautiful, exotic looking, young woman. Paige had to give her props for her style and the look she pulled off effortlessly. Tamala had long, silky, natural hair that stop in the middle of her back. Her skin was light, and her almond eyes, with irises that were so dark they appeared to be black, caused Tamala's ethnicity to be in question.

Tamala Sykes was fierce. If Paige had been a lesser woman, she could have been intimidated by this beauty's presence. But she wasn't and decided to ignore the shade Tamala threw her way each visit. Although it seemed this time Tamala's tone was icier than usual as she confirmed her next appointment. Paige compared her to a little robot, only doing what she was being paid to do by the members of Liberty Church.

Paige wanted to put the chic in her place when Tamala didn't even say "Have a nice day", but dismissed her with a "That will be all." It was as if she thought she was Meryl Streep in *The Devil Wears Prada*, and she,

Paige, was Anne Hathaway. Paige held her resolve not to release her anger on this receptionist. She simply said, "Thank you Sister Sykes," and made her way out of the office. On her way out, she smiled at her ability to walk away from that underserved rudeness and cold shoulder. In the words of Elsa, who she was now fond of thanks to Nikki, "The cold never bothered her anyway."

*** 

"Camille did you speak to Karen about that family issue?" Benjamin asked. He was holding the dustpan as she swept the kitchen floor. Everyone had left shortly after Nikki's scare. They had just received word that Nikki was in the bed asleep for the night.

"No Benjamin, we kind of had a health crisis here tonight."

"But there was plenty of time before that, when you two were in the basement alone."

"We were putting away the gifts, and besides Tabitha and Dawn were helping as well."

"That's why you invited them right?" Ben asked with one eyebrow raised. Camille thought it was the cutest thing ever. She couldn't help but smile as she put away the broom and he threw the trash in the waste basket.

"Ben, I know I have been dragging my feet. I will tell her soon, okay? Let's not fight about it again, please." Ben walked to her and gave her a hug. They lingered in the embrace for a long moment; he pulled back and placed a kiss on her lips. He promptly moved to her forehead, placing a kiss there. It was safer than on her delicious lips. He stepped away with her hands still in his.

"Cam, I don't want to fight with you. I want you to be happy. It is my job to keep you that way. That means sometimes when you get in the way of your own happiness, I have to call you out on it. I don't want you to allow fear to make you continue procrastinating. Karen loves you and I don't think for a second she will blame you for J.D.'s actions. However, the longer you wait the more culpable you will be in hurting her. You feel me?" Ben pulled her to his masculine body and Camille melted into his warmth. She knew he was right. She had to tell Karen but she needed to make sure Nikki was healthy first.

"I will tell her once I know Nikki is okay. They are taking her to the doctor tomorrow morning before Karen comes in to the office. I will tell her when she arrives and I am sure Nikki will be fine, health wise."

"You promise?" Ben asked.

"I promise."

Ben hugged her tighter, kissed her gently on her lips, and began to sway with her in a slow dance without music. He started to sing in her ear with his soul-stirring baritone voice, the lyrics of Ed Sheeran's "Thinking Out Loud." Camille wrapped her arms around his neck and placed her head on his beating heart as the song commanded. She enjoyed the lyrics of loving one another with longevity. She was beyond impressed with Ben's ability to sing Acapella. Benjamin was not only an astute businessman but he was musically gifted. He could play the piano and guitar, and often did while singing to her. Tonight he chose to serenade her with his melodic voice. She concentrated on the words he sang smoothly in her ear.

They were words so true to them. They fell in love in such a mysterious way. From the first conversation she had with Ben at her desk he had her heart; and the way he stayed by her side after she was hit by an SUV and endured critical injuries, secured it. Benjamin stayed with her despite all the objections she threw his way. He had helped Karen during the crisis and volunteered at her company, helping to bring on top accounts. This man was a godsend and an answer to prayers she had yet to pray. Ben's love and actions made her fall in love with him every day. Some might say they were moving too fast but she knew it was meant to last.

When he made it to the phrase, referring to being kissed under the stars, she was done. She did not know if her resolve to abstain from yielding her body to him would hold strong tonight. But Ben, being the gentleman, gave her a hug and separated their bodies to a safe distance. He gently pulled her by the hand.

"Come on let's get you packed up so I can take you home. It's getting harder and harder to break away from you. How long do we have until our wedding day?"

Camille was happy he changed the course of the evening. She felt ashamed she had not been the one to put on the breaks. Without making eye contact, she addressed his question.

"Let's see…" Camille picked up her phone and scanned the calendar. "Today is September 8th —we will marry on November 1. We have eight weeks until we are husband and wife."

Benjamin picked Camille up and twirled her around. "Ms. James, I can't wait eight weeks for you to become Mrs. Benjamin George Adams. Let's just go to the courthouse and do this thing. The bible says it's better to marry than burn, and I'm like an oven on high. I am beginning to smell smoke around here. What do you say?"

Camille laughed at Benjamin until she realized he was not joking. "Ben we haven't attended a counseling session yet, and besides I want to walk down the aisle. I may not be his biggest fan right now, but he is still my dad and he deserves to give me away."

"Camille, there is nothing in those sessions that will stop me from marrying you. We can still have the wedding afterwards so Mr. James can have the honor of giving me what I already know is mine. The point is, we would be married and no longer have a need for you to leave our home so I can keep my hands off you."

Camille shook her head as she pulled on her light jacket. With the change of season, the temperature was much cooler in the evenings during September in Memphis. "Benjamin, no we are sticking to our plan. Now come on and take me home. We will not be eloping, we have a plan and we will follow it. We are so close, no need to ruin it by losing focus."

Ben shrugged as he grabbed his keys off the bar. "Can't blame a guy for trying."

***

Paige was drying off after a long hot shower; she was feeling optimistic about being able to have her rough edges smoothed out through therapy. She looked at the woman in the mirror as she applied moisturizer to her hair and moved to the cocoa butter oil she used on her body. She had thought it had been a slow start for her in counseling, but she was proud of herself for opening up to Dr. Whitney. Allowing anyone to view the dark enigmas that she possessed was perplexing. Paige had to fight with vehemence against her personal demons—happiness and love were worth the fight. Paige completed her nightly beauty regime and slipped into her favorite "I love Paris" pajamas. She was headed to bed, notebook in hand, to read the scriptures Dr. Whitney suggested when her doorbell rang.

Paige opened the door and was accosted by a distraught Kevin. She was petrified when he grabbed her by the waist and lifted her up to straddle his body. He wailed into the crook of her neck. His grip on her was so unyielding that Paige responded by prying his hands off her waist. After a slight tussle, she managed to free herself from his stronghold. She stepped back, looked into his lifeless eyes and immediately went back to him, reaching out to wipe his falling tears. *She had never seen Kevin cry.* While she embraced him, Kevin dropped the side of his face into the palm of her hand and allowed her to caress him. Paige realized the door to her apartment was open, but she managed to close it without losing contact. After a weighty pause, Paige began. "Kevin, tell me what is wrong. What's going on babe?"

Kevin didn't want to talk; he needed to be assured that giving up his relationship with his mother was worth the sacrifice. He didn't want words from her lips, he wanted action. Paige attempted to speak again, but he caught the words with his mouth. The kiss was obsessive as he released his anguish, frustration, and grief with the connection of his lips and body to hers. Paige desperately wanted to know what caused Kevin to be this vulnerable. Was it a case? She thought. Had he lost in court? No, he was off today he went to Atlanta to—HIS MOTHER. Paige attempted to pull away. Kevin tightened his hold and finally spoke.

"Please Paige I need you. I need this; I'm incomplete without you... without us!" Paige surrendered to her man. Only the Lord knew her heart, and she could not break Kevin's by denying him what he seemed to be pleading for. She would comfort him, because he loved her flaws and all. She knew she was a jigsaw puzzle with missing pieces, a Rubik's cube without all the colors, a scavenger hunt without any clues. She was determined to love this man, and allow his love to adorn her.

Kevin felt her relent to his will and lifted Paige by the waist. She voluntarily wrapped her legs around his body and whispered in his ear, "Let's get something to drink." He turned left to go into the kitchen, and held Paige at an angle so she could grab a bottle of wine out of the wine rack, and glasses out of her cabinet. They stumbled to her bedroom where Kevin placed her on her feet. She undressed, found her music player and picked "Kevin's Love Songs" playlist, while he prepared their liquid courage. Kevin smiled as he walked to Paige and gave her the glass of wine. The first song she played was enforcement to his rising libido, the voice was Beyoncé, and the words were a soothing balm to his tortured spirit. He understood his lady had issues, but she was working on them. If she fell along the way, while on her journey of recovery he would be there to catch her. He truly loved her flaws and all. He sipped his glass of wine, while the song filled the bedroom, and looked intensely into his lover's eyes. He accepted the lyrics to the song as confirmation; his china doll was worth the sacrifice. When the next song played it was K. Michelle, belting out "V.S.O.P." Kevin adorned his complex, frustrating, and unpredictable lady with love throughout the night. They were both resolved to the night of passion, before dealing with the cause of his devastation in the morning.

***

Carol Steele was a woman full of grief and despair that would not let go of her thoughts and her very soul. She sat in Lauren's childhood bedroom looking at all the awards, degrees, and pictures from her only child's youth. Lauren had been her world, her pride, and her joy. She was loving, kind, devoted, and in Carol's mind, taken away from this Earth too soon. Carol picked up a frame that held a collage of pictures of Lauren. Some were of her as an infant, growing to a toddler, then school age, and all the way up to her life with Benjamin.

It wasn't long ago, that she blamed Benjamin for not making Lauren a mother and a wife. She could not understand how he was now ready to commit to this girl he had just met barely a year ago. Oh, how she wanted him to suffer the way she suffered, knowing she would never be the mother of a bride or a grandmother. Just thinking of never being called Nana or Me-Me made her feel hopeless. Recently, she started attending therapy sessions with the support of her friend, and Benjamin's mother, Ellen. After a few sessions, she started to realize that it wasn't Benjamin's fault; he had a right to move on.  He was after all still in the land of the living. Dr. Whitney was able to help her see how wrong she had been in trying to keep Benjamin in the mourning stage of grief as she was. She grimaced as she recalled the therapy session where she reached the epiphany that she was wrong in her view of Benjamin's relationship.

*Carol sat across from Dr. Whitney with her best-friend Ellen Adams, who had been holding her hand the entire session. Carol was deep in thought trying to give the doctor an answer to her question.*

*"Carol, when you saw Benjamin propose to Camille, how did you feel?" After what seemed a long time, she finally spoke.*

*"I didn't understand how he could do that to my baby. Proposing marriage to that girl, when he never gave Lauren a promise ring. Do you know how many nights my*

*baby girl cried in my arms about that man? She wanted
nothing more than to be his wife and the mother of his
children."*

*Dr. Whitney turned to Carol. "That is what you
thought about Benjamin's proposal to Camille; now tell me
how you felt about it." Carol sighed, she closed her eyes as
she let go of Ellen's hand and let her neck fall back in
exasperation. She then took another deep breath, opened
her eyes, and looked at the four piercing ones staring back
at her.*

*"I felt violated by Benny proposing to that girl,
after knowing her for such a short time. When he was
saying how strong she was, my chest tightened and my
stomach churned. I felt anger like never before and I
wanted to stop Benny from making a mistake. I don't
remember what I thought or felt after that. That is when my
mind went black because my anger turned into rage, and I
picked up that skillet determined to knock some sense into
that boy."*

*As soon as those words left her mouth, Carol looked
to her best friend and realized how she admittedly hurt this
lady's son, and here she sat with her. She felt remorse at
that very moment, followed by an understanding that her*

*hurt had manifested into anger and she had allowed herself to become a monster. She immediately apologized to Ellen for hurting her son. Ellen being the woman of grace forgave her and simply said, "Carol you must forgive yourself and allow Dr. Whitney with the Lord, to help you heal."*

Now she was ashamed of her actions and her treatment of Camille. But the tightness in her chest didn't ease with this revelation. The hole in heart seemed only to grow because she understood if she was to continue on, she had to let go and make amends. The only issue she had with that was how to do it.

She rose from the desk where her daughter once did her homework and wrote a thesis statement to obtain a Master's Degree, and went to her bed. There once was a time when she could lay on this bed and smell Lauren's scent. Lauren always visited one weekend, every month. She had just been home the weekend prior to her being taken. While Lauren's scent was still there, it was as if she had a piece of her. The day she no longer could smell the sweet scent of her daughter, was the day the pain came down on her like a wrecking ball. She understood she needed to let go of the anger, pain, and resentment and to make true amends with Benjamin and Camille. Ultimately, she was resolved that this was what she was going to do. In the meantime, Carol felt weary and had to lie down in Lauren's bed, on her back with the picture frame clutched to her bosom and wept until slumber took over.

Gregory Steele turned off the television after watching his favorite religious program. He proceeded to turn down all the lights and set the alarm system of his home. He went to the master bedroom and prepared to turn in with his beloved, only he was grieved to see she was not in their room. There was only one other place she would be. He turned around defeated and headed to Lauren's room. His heart was heavy because Lauren had been gone for almost two years now. His beloved wife still grieved the same as the moment they heard the doctor deliver the news. He missed his baby girl too, not a day went by when he didn't think of her, but his memories were a balm to his sorrow, sadly there was no soothing his beloved.

He thought back to a few months after Lauren's death. He had tried to change Lauren's bedroom to a study. He did not want his wife to make the room into a shrine for her grief. Her reaction to that suggestion allowed him to see his wife was only a vicious shell of the beautiful doll he'd married.

*"Doll let's turn the spare bedroom into a study, where we can pray and read the bible together. You know it could be our own prayer closet."*

*"Are you crazy! That is not a spare bedroom. It's Lauren's. Now you listen to me well, before I let you touch that room I will divorce you."*

*Gregory tried to make light of the situation to calm her down. "Doll, you know we are married until death do us part." He gave her that old charming smile that calmed her for the last four decades. Her next statements proved the charm was gone.*

*"Gregory Steele, I would kill you dead before I so much as let you paint my baby's wall." He never broached the topic again.*

After that, he began to fast and pray, and continued to this day without ceasing, that his wife's grief would be lifted from her. He was out of options. If Dr. Whitney could not help her, then who could? Gregory had stopped trying to talk to her about their daughter and just prayed that a breakthrough would come their way.

He went into Lauren's room, his heart broke yet again to see his beloved's face puffy, and tear stained. He removed the picture from her clutches and lifted her body to carry her into their bedroom. He undressed her and put her into her nightgown, and tucked her gently into bed. He then kneeled beside her on his knees and prayed in Jesus's name for the mending of a fragile heart.

## *Chapter 3*
## *The Morning After*

Kevin woke up in a fog. Rubbing the sleep from his eyes he sat up, looking around wondering where he was. He realized he was in Paige's bedroom with no Paige in sight; panic struck him in the pit of his stomach. He jumped up, and picked up his pants that were folded and put neatly on her bedroom chair. Kevin hoped she was okay with the events of last night; he was on a quest to find her.  He remembered what Frankie had said about Karen after they made love once, after she *'got saved.'* Kevin did not want a repeat of that episode starring Paige. He looked in her in-suite bathroom—empty. He dashed down her short hallway into the living room and glanced around to her study area— No Paige.  Frustrated he rubbed his hands over his wavy, fade haircut, and tried to think of her morning habits.

"Think Kevin think." He hoped she had not run off, waiting on him to leave before she returned. He went into the kitchen thinking she would need her morning joe to get going. If there was some made, he might stand a chance. Entering the kitchen his heart leaped with joy, she had left a note on the counter.

*Babe,*

*I wanted to make us breakfast, no food shot that plan down (lol). I went to grab something, be back in a few.*

*Love Ya!*

*P.S. I know you are off today, so I called in to the office letting them know I will take the day off. That way we have the entire day together.*

Kevin audibly exhaled. His girl was no weakling, she doesn't run. Smiling, he headed back to the bedroom to shower and prepare for breakfast, and the conversation they didn't have last night.

\*\*\*

Karen held Nikki's hand as the nurse labeled her back with numbers for the allergy test. Nikki was being such a big girl. She was being brave and holding still. Karen tried to focus solely on being there for her baby girl and ignore the bile that was starting to rise in the back of her throat, caused by Frankie stepping out of the patient's room to talk to Dawn about Shayla.

Every day Shayla was contacting Frankie directly or through the girls with some issue. She could kick herself for not knowing Shayla was still on his government insurance. They still shared credit cards and a joint banking account as well. Who does that? She had made the discovery as she was adding her financial and legal documents into their now shared file cabinet and came across his.  Frankie hadn't asked her yet how she felt about his shared assets with his former wife. She tried to convince herself it didn't matter. Karen had a great plan with ITS and it shouldn't be a big deal, *right*?  Karen understood blending their families would require the patience of a saint, but how much patience should a saint have? Their daughter could've died last night and Frankie was in the hall discussing who knows what concerning his ex-wife. She had no doubt it concerned Shayla, if it was about one of the girls he would have stayed in the room. Being married to a man who was best friends with his ex was not ideal. Karen was pulled out of her thoughts, as the door opened and Frankie walked in all smiles.

"How is daddy's girl doing?" Frankie's question caused Nikki to move to see him. The nurse looked up with a frown of agitation. Karen, scolded Frankie.

"Frankie, Nikki has to hold still, she can't move."

"I'm sorry," he whispered. "Daddy didn't mean to make you move. Be still like mommy and the nurse said." Nikki shut her eyes tight, as her dad told her what a brave girl she was being and that he would be taking her to eat

whatever she wanted after this. Karen rolled her eyes
toward the heavens.

"Frankie you can't promise her that. We don't know
what she is allergic to." Karen was sick of Frankie and
wished she had come alone. First, he was in and out dealing
with his ex-wife's issues. Now he was in here confusing
her child.

"Karen I'm sorry. I keep putting my foot in my
mouth, I'm nervous."

"About what, Nikki or something with the former
Mrs. Jones?"

"Karen, of course with Nikki. Shayla is just tripping
about some accounts I'm closing and trying to keep
insurance coverage. Why Dawn called me about it, I don't
know. But I handled it."

"Sure you did, until the next crisis or whatever she
feels like griping about." Karen's tone was so hostile it
shocked him; he had never heard her voice filled with so
much contempt.

Frankie looked at Karen bewildered. "Are we
seriously going to fight while Nikki is being prepped for
this procedure?" He raised an eyebrow at her.

"I'm not fighting; I just don't understand you and Shayla. But we can talk about it later. Looks like they are about to start injecting her."

Frankie grimaced as he watched the nurse pull needles from what looked like small ice tray packs and put the needles into Nikki's back. Each section of the tray held various foods and environmental substances to determine what she was allergic to.

Nikki began to cry and complain about her back itching and burning. She began kicking and trying to grab the nurse's hand to bring a stop to her anguish. Frankie was summoned to hold her feet as Karen held down her upper body. This was not how he wanted their marriage and family to start. It had been one dramatic event after another. He wanted to make Karen happy and keep Nikki safe, and love them as they both deserved. However, Shayla was not making it easy and he could tell Karen was struggling with keeping her cool.

Frankie was annoyed by his earlier phone call just as much as Karen was. Dawn was doing her mother's bidding, she texted him *9-1-1*, which meant he had to call her immediately to talk. As he listened to Dawn, he realized he would have to clarify what constituted a *9-1-1* text. Shayla's insurance coverage was not one of them. Shayla

had been diagnosed with Lupus over five years ago and
Frankie let her remain on his insurance after the divorce.
Shayla hadn't had a flare up in years, but had put Dawn up
to begging him not to remove her from his family plan.
Shayla insisted that as a hairstylist she didn't know if the
disease would allow her to continue in her profession. He
promised his daughter he would consider it, which meant
discussing it with Karen, but thought it was best not to
bring her name up. He didn't want the girls to associate
anything negative regarding Shayla with Karen. Although
he knew if he didn't rid his life of all things Shayla, his new
marriage may end before it truly began.

When he and Shayla divorced, they were supposed
to split all their assets in half. They hadn't completed the
court order. Looking back that was irresponsible of them,
but hindsight always has twenty-twenty vision. However,
back then Shayla and he were on such good terms that
whatever he had, he freely shared with her. Now things
were different, he was married. The entire situation with
the bank accounts and insurance was giving him heartburn
and a headache.

Frankie turned his attention to Karen. She was
rubbing Nikki's hair with one hand and holding her little
hands with the other. She was speaking softly to their

daughter, soothing her as only a loving mother could. Dear God, she was beautiful. Her long, shiny, black hair; her modest but stunning look was one to behold. She was all he wanted and everything he needed. He had to make this work; he had to get Shayla's demands under control before Karen was fed up.   He was brought out of his reverie when he heard a small whimpering voice.

"Daddy, can you come up here with me and mommy? I won't kick anymore I promise."

"Of course sweet-pea daddy is here with you."

"My back hurts."

Frankie leaned around her to view her back. She had purple whelps and knots all over her skin. It appeared every injection had some type of reaction. Frankie had never seen anything like it before. Guilt started to creep in, was this caused by her being conceived by parents who were intoxicated with alcohol and drugs?  No, he couldn't wallow in dooming thoughts. He squeezed Nikki's hand and lowered to whisper in her ear.

"You are being such a brave girl. This will all be over soon and we will know what causes all the itching and burning. Can you continue being brave a little longer?"

Nikki nodded yes, and squeezed her daddy's hand and gripped her mom's tighter. She was so happy God had answered her prayer and let her have a mommy and a daddy.

Karen smiled with delight as she watched Frankie calm Nikki. This felt right. She would try to be more patient. She couldn't imagine going through this with just Nikki and herself.

The doctor and nurse came back into the room. The nurse had liquid medicine she explained was an antihistamine that would stop Nikki's discomfort.

Nikki took the medicine and began to drink. All the adults in the room saw her cute face turn into a mean frown. She closed her eyes tight and her lips became a straight line, then she spat the medicine out. It landed on the doctor's white jacket. She threw the cup that contained the rest of the medicine and it hit the wall. She started to cry while she screamed.

"That medicine is nasty; I hate it here!" She fell to the floor kicking her feet and wailing as she was in pain and now her throat hurt and her stomach burned from the inside out. The medicine tasted like bitter fire.

It took several minutes for her parents to calm her. The doctor ordered an injection of the medicine, and it took all of the adults to hold Nikki down, as she became the little patient of horror.

Twenty minutes later, the doctor was able to explain the test results and Karen's heart dropped to her shoes. She listened as the doctor described her child's life-threatening allergies. Some were environmental and others were food.

Nikki was allergic to cedar trees, redwood trees, Bermuda grass, weeds, dust, mold, dogs, cats, shellfish, peanuts, cashews, peaches, and strawberries. She would be on four daily medicines to combat the symptoms, and would have to see the allergist once a quarter.

Both Frankie and Karen had heavy hearts as they asked question after question. The doctor was patient and answered all their concerns. He assured them that Nikki did not have the worst-case reactions and she could grow out of the symptoms. Her medical condition was termed urticaria and they were given booklets to read and websites to visit to learn more about caring for a child with the illness.

The Jones family left the Medical Specialist building, and headed out to treat Nikki with food she could eat from her favorite restaurant. Afterwards, Frankie would drop Karen off at work and keep Nikki home for the remainder of the day.

Karen was looking up urticaria on her phone as she rode on the passenger's side. Nikki had fallen asleep in the back after more tears were shed about it not being fair that she couldn't eat whatever she wanted, play in grass, and climb trees. However, it was the tears she shed about wanting a puppy and a cat for her birthday that caused Karen to cry along with her child. Frankie had to pull over at a gas station to console them both. He had been their rock and Karen felt guilty for wishing he had not come with them. She leaned over and gave him a kiss and whispered "I love you." That momentarily eased all the tension between them and the tumultuous morning they had endured.

Karen's attention was on one of the medical websites the doctor had given them; she was planning a course of action on caring for Nikki. Frankie called her name breaking into her thoughts. She looked up from her phone expectantly.

"Karen, I need to talk to you about some things concerning Sheila. Some bank accounts and credit cards."

"I'm aware of them and her medical insurance coverage. I saw them when I was filing my and Nikki's important documents."

"Why didn't you say something?"

"I didn't think it was something I should have to approach you for. I was waiting on you to share it with me. Now that you have, please continue."

Frankie cleared his throat and began concentrating on merging onto Interstate 240.  Karen thought once he was on the interstate he who would continue, but he didn't. This was a growing irritation for her.  Frankie could not just spit anything out; he had all these commercial breaks during conversations.

"Go on Frankie, finish what you were saying. How much is in these accounts you never closed as your divorce settlement declared you to?"

Frankie cleared his throat and nervously glanced over at her with an inquisitive look. Karen understood what he was asking how she knew what the divorce settlement decreed.

"I read your divorce settlement. Don't look so surprised. It's clear you are

not offering up information, so I have to snoop, which I resent, to find out what I need to know. So please tell me how much."

"Six-hundred thousand dollars."  Karen dropped her phone.

"What the…" she had not seen documents for accounts that had that much money. "How can a mail carrier have that type of money?"

\*\*\*

Camille was dividing her attention between revisions to a contract from the legal department of a new retail account, and samples of dresses for her bridesmaids sent over by the same retailer. She was signing off on the contract as Debra her clerical manager buzzed in on her phone.

"Ms. James, there is a Carol Steele on line three for you."

Camille picked up the receiver. "Thanks Debra, I will take the call, please come and pick up these signed contracts and have them delivered to the legal team."

"Yes, Ma'am."

Camille couldn't think of one reason Mrs. Carol should be calling her. However, there was only one way to find out, Camille pressed the blinking button for line three.

"I.T.S., Camille James speaking."

"Hi Camille, this is Carol… Carol Steele"

"Hi Mrs. Carol, how are you?" She really wanted to say, "Why on earth would you be calling me at my office?" However, she just waited for the purpose of the call in silence.

"I'm doing fine. I just wanted to call and say I—I'm sorry. You know, sorry about all the drama I've caused you and Benny. I didn't mean you any harm. The Lord knows I love Benny like he's my own. I just miss my baby girl so much."

Camille heard Mrs. Carol's moans and was stunned by the emotional outpour from her. She had no idea how to respond to this apology. *Think Camille, Think!*

"Mrs. Carol, please don't cry. I forgive you, I understand you are hurting and still in the grieving process. I just want you to know, I'm not trying to replace your daughter or erase her memory. I love Benjamin and accept you as a part of his family; I just want you to give me a chance." Camille waited for a response. She could sense Mrs. Carol was trying to calm her emotions.

"Thanks for your forgiveness. I just want you to know you won't be having any more problems from me."

"Don't worry about it, I appreciate you calling. Is there anything I can do for you?"

"No, I just wanted to say, I was sorry about hitting Benny with that skillet, and being downright evil to you for no reason."

"I accept your apology and hope we can get to know each other."

"It's all in God's hands now. Thanks for taking my call. I will be getting off now."

"All right then, Mrs. Carol. Take care."

Camille placed the receiver down on the base. Chills went down her spine. Mrs. Carol's disposition was odd. Before she could ponder more about the call, Debra came in to her office. Debra had been an employee of I.T.S for two years. She began as a clerical staff member. Her attention to detail and magnetic personality earned her the manager role. Debra was a petite, caramel-skinned, middle-aged woman that did not appear a day over thirty-five. Her kind heart and gentle spirit was allowing her to age gracefully. When it came to Camille, Karen, and I.T.S though, she was a pit-bull that wanted every i dotted and t crossed. She was currently enrolled in college pursuing a marketing degree. Camille had convinced her it was never too late to earn a degree, or anything else in life she wanted. That was one of the reasons she loved working for Camille. She pushed her employees to be the best at I.T.S and in life. Debra entered the office with a smile on her face and pep in her step.

"Hi Debra, you look wonderful this morning. I love that haircut."

"Thanks Camille, I was going for something new with this short cut. You know they say that as we get older short hair makes you look more youthful. I'm trying to stay as young as I can. I know husband number two is out there waiting for me, so I got to be ready child."

"Debra, are you ready?" They both fell into laughter. Camille picked up the signed contracts and motioned for Debra to take them. "These are the contracts that should be couriered to our legal team. We are ready to go with this retailer."

Debra took the envelope with pride. "I'll be happy to send them. I am so proud of you and this business. This account makes one hundred and fifteen companies we distribute for."

Debra did a happy dance that let anyone know she was of the Pentecostal Faith. She threw her hands up and screamed Hallelujah, then followed by speaking in tongues. Another reason Debra loved I.T.S., was because Camille let you praise the Lord in her fancy office while she clapped, creating the shouting music. After their praise break, Debra gathered Camille in her arms and gave her a tight hug. Camille hugged back just as tightly and said, "Thank you, but it's all you employees that make it possible."

"That's what I love about you. You are always including us in your success." Debra was an emotional woman who could cry on cue, and that is what she did. Camille gave her a minute to get it out before ending their praise and worship.

"No more crying Ms. Debra. We are a team, and I appreciate you for your work ethic and loyalty. Now dry those eyes and let's get back to business."

Debra whimpered and stepped out of the embrace. She got her emotions under control and said, "Yes ma'am, I'm on it."

After Debra exited the office, Camille gave a silent prayer of gratitude to the Lord for increasing her territory. She prayed that she would continue her career with humbleness, and vowed always to give Him the glory for it all belonged to Him. When she sat down and she called Benjamin to inform him of her peculiar call with Mrs. Carol, another matter she was optimistic was coming to a close with victory. She dialed his number. He picked up on the second ring.

"Love, how are you this morning?"

Blushing, Camille responded. "I'm doing well. Sweetie this morning has gotten off to a great start."

"Oh yeah, tell me about it."

"I received a call from Mrs. Carol and she apologized, saying she would not be giving us any more problems."

"That's great, Cam. Maybe counseling is helping her."

"Has to be, she has never been nice to me."

"Well we thank the Lord for her change of attitude. I see why you sound so upbeat; I can hear your smile through the phone."

"You hear a smile because I'm talking to the man I love, and I just sent another signed contract to legal. An account I earned from the recommendation of my future husband."

"Ah, so it's a done deal, huh?"

"Yes, thanks to you. I don't know how I will ever repay you."

"Oh sweetheart, you have the rest of your life." Ben said slyly.

"Benjamin, be good." Camille could never get over her schoolgirl blush with this guy.

"Honey, I am good and I'm proud of you. I only referred the client you closed the deal. It's my job to keep supplying all things that will keep you happy in every area of your life."

"Ben, that means so much to me. I love you, but I won't keep you on the phone. I know you are busy and I'm expecting Karen at any moment."

"I love you too. Call me if you need me after you talk to her. I'm here for you."

"I know you are, talk to you later."

Camille ended the call and smiled. She could not believe this was her life. Not even a year ago, her life was work and more work. She didn't have a social life outside of corporate events. She spent most evenings alone and reading fictional romance stories. Then Benjamin came into her life making her fantasies, reality. She stopped and thought about how differently things could have turned out.

It was their first date and as she attempted to cross the street to the theater, she was hit by a SUV. She spent the first couple of months of their relationship recovering, however Ben didn't stop his pursuit of courting her. He was there at the hospital when she came out of brain surgery and had been by her side almost every day since. Fortunately, the hit and run driver did not get away with almost killing her. She had Frankie to thank for that. He had been instrumental in helping Kevin gain the evidence that put the drunk driver behind bars for a several years. Prayerfully, Brian Andrews was getting the help he needed

so when his time was served he would come out a better
individual. Her thoughts went back to her man. Oh how she
loved him! She never knew she could love so strongly, but
she did and was better for it.

She picked up her wedding magazines and
samples, smiling while giving them her undivided
attention. She chose Paige's and Karen's dress and emailed
them the link to view it online. Her attention was turned to
a knock on her door. Camille swallowed. She knew it was
Karen on the other side. It was time to confess.

***

Kevin had showered and gotten dressed by the time
Paige came in with breakfast. She had gone to one of their
favorite cafes, Momma Gladys's Home Cooking. The
owner Gladys was a great cook with an even better sense of
humor.  She could have been on tour as stand-up comedian.
Kevin thought Paige looked adorable in her pink fleece
warm-up and snickers. Her hair was in a high, bouncy
ponytail. Paige was busy setting their plates and was
oblivious to Kevin's assessment of her. He hoped like crazy
they could work out the kinks in their relationship; living
without her was not an option for him. His firecracker was
busy making sure the food was warm and arranged just so.

She had that OCD quality that meant she needed things like her plate, silverware, and glass to be in a particular arrangement. It was humorous how she would change the setting everywhere they dined to meet her standards. She couldn't focus until it was her way. Kevin just stood there and watched her. She was beautiful. He couldn't believe he almost gave her up for his mother's prejudices. It was still a mystery why Paige set off his mother's hatred bells. However, he had solved the case that Paige was the thief of his heart, thoughts, and desires.

Paige finally had the breakfast in order and felt his penetrating stare. She smiled with her eyes and winked. He had been caught feasting on her as she prepared their meal.

"Come on honey let's eat." Kevin took the seat across from Paige and they held hands to say prayer.

Kevin loved Momma Gladys's Ham, Eggs, white rice, and biscuits. It was the best southern breakfast in the Mid-South. Paige had oatmeal, turkey bacon, a blueberry muffin, and a yogurt parfait. They ate in silence for a while until Paige finally spoke.

"So will you be sharing with me what happened in Atlanta? What happened down there to have you bum-rushing in here like you did last night?" Paige put her fork in her plate and looked up at Kevin for an answer.

Kevin sighed and rubbed his hand through his hair. He picked up his glass of orange juice and swallowed a big gulp. He looked up into those mystical, brown eyes of Paige's and saw she was patiently waiting for a reply.

"Paige, sweetheart… I don't know where to start." Kevin sat back in his chair, leaned his head back, and closed his eyes. He wanted to be honest without hurting her. That always led to Raige.

Paige was growing impatient waiting. Obviously, he could not answer her inquiry without assistance. "When you went to your parents' were they both home?"

"Yes."

"What happened when you were there, did you talk to them about us?"

"Not at first. Mother insisted we have dinner."

Typical, Paige thought. Julia was always trying to simulate being the embodiment of southern charm and hospitality. She cleared those thoughts from her mind. She was hoping her questions would lead Kevin into divulging the rest on his own. So far, no such luck. She was going to have to pull every detail out of him.

"Did you talk during dinner, about us being together?"

"Yes."

Ok, finally we are getting somewhere. "How did they take it?"

"Mother did not take it well at all. She went ballistic and threatened to file charges against you, as usual dad said nothing."

"Oh my God, can she do that…do I need to get an attorney?" Paige was now coming undone; her heart was beating so rapidly against her chest she grabbed at it with her open palm. It felt like it would beat out of her body. She could barely hear Kevin. He was still speaking, she knew because she saw his mouth moving, but none of his words were audible. Had she finally gone too far when she attacked Julia? She had it coming for speaking so vile about her mom, and then spitting in her face—Paige only remembered blacking out now. Oh God, please don't let me go to jail, I am working on myself, and I'm getting better. Paige silently prayed in her head. Her thoughts were racing from one conclusion to the next without any pause in between. Did Kevin come over to give her pity sex and then break the news that he was going to prosecute her? Abruptly, his voice became audible again and her heart shattered into pieces as the words vomited out of his mouth.

"Mother said you were not welcome in her home, and I informed her that neither was I. Dad just sat there as I was banned from our home, it was awful. It took everything in me to make it from Atlanta to your door."

Paige quickly rose from her seat and went to Kevin; he pushed his chair back allowing her room to sit. She straddled his lap, looking into his eyes and searching his soul. He held her gaze allowing her to search, as he was wide open for her to understand how much she meant to him.

"Kev, are you sure you want to do this…be estranged from your parents?"

"Paige, I. Am. Not. Losing. You. I Won't. Give. You. Up." Kevin grabbed the sides of her face and kissed her. The kiss was full of emotion—the unspoken hurt of severing ties with his mother, the deep connection he felt with Paige. It seemed to go on for forever. Kevin was first to break the contact lifting her off his lap. Paige looked down at him confused.

"What…why did you stop?"

"Paige, I didn't choose you just for sex, I…What about your therapy and spiritual process?"

Irritated and feeling rejected she snapped back. "What about it?" She went back to her seat, picked up her purified water, and drank with eyebrows raised over her glass.

Kevin chose to ignore the sarcastic look Paige gave him. "How did your session go yesterday?"

"Fine."

"Come on babe, don't be like that. I've attended the single's ministry class and know we were wrong for making love last night. I don't want to be a 'stumbling block' for you on your spiritual journey."

"Oh I see, the morning after you sex me all night. Are you ready for me to be holy now?" Paige was insulted by his comment regarding her spiritual life. It was a fine time for him to think about it after he released in her too many times to count throughout the night.

"Paige, you are taking it all wrong. I'm new with this Christian walk. Yesterday I felt empty and needed you. Maybe we should have prayed or fasted, but I wanted— needed your comfort. I always want you but I know that can't continue to happen and we stay on this journey. Nor do I want you to have a setback and feel remorse for making love to me, ever!"

"Kevin, I'm not Karen. I will not be having an emotional breakdown because we screwed. To answer your question about therapy, it went better than fine. I was able to release a lot that has been pinned up in my heart since I was a little girl. Dr. Whitney is great, she can get me to open up and see myself. I mean really see myself and why I do the things, I do. She also reiterates that being a Christian is a process. I'm not going to always get it right, and neither are you. But that doesn't mean I don't love the Lord and that I'm off the path to recovery. The Lord knows my heart and loves me just the same. Dr. Whitney said we are dealing with my internal issues before we get to all the do's and don'ts of being saved." Paige's features and voice softened. "But, thank you for putting the brakes on before. I admit I was feeling rejected and lashed out. I should not have done that but you are right. Although, I have not committed to celibacy it isn't the answer to every emotional episode we have."

"Wow sweetie, I don't know what to say. You sound so....so...therapeutic. I'm proud of you and I'm on this journey with you. Okay?"

Paige gave him that dazzling smile he loved. "Okay, let's finish this delicious Momma Gladys's breakfast. She wants me to call her and tell her how we enjoyed it"

As Kevin dug back into his plate, he felt like Adele. *"If this ain't love, then what is"?* He *was willing to take the risk.*

## *Chapter 4*
## *Fragile Hearts*

*Benjamin's*

Benjamin was in his home gym on the treadmill doing an afternoon run. His pace was fast at 10.0 and he was pushing the incline button to raise the resistance to level five. The sweat pouring from his skin was hot and salty; it fell from his body onto the treadmill's belt like a puddle of rain. Nonetheless, the endorphins circulating through his system were exhilarating. He was running up a steep incline to release the pressure of his morning.

His vice president had called and delivered solemn news that he had the responsibility of laying off five members of his team. That wasn't going to be easy, everyone on his team had a family to support. Why the lay-offs? The company was profitable. Ben had received a six-digit bonus last month for the growth of his territory in sales. If given the choice, he would gladly give it back for everyone on his team to remain employed. However, he was not the final decision maker, and he must end the career of five of his team members. To release his fury, he was running as fast as he could up a tough hill. This was how he dealt with the disappointment he felt in his role in cutthroat corporate America.

He ran as fast as he could on an incline level that was causing his calf muscles to protest. They burned, but he ran. His shins were screaming for mercy, but he ran until there was ringing in his ears. The need to release anxiety and frustration would not allow him to slow. He ran until the ringing became louder and louder. Suddenly he realized it was the actual doorbell.

Who would come to his home in the late afternoon without calling? It wasn't Camille. She had an entry code to his alarm system programed in her mobile device and she would not ring the doorbell, she would just walk in calling his name. He smiled at the thought of her voice as he reluctantly pressed down on his incline button and came to a slow walk. He grudgingly got off his stress reliever. Grabbing a towel and bottle of water, he made his way to the front door.

Looking out the window, he saw Mrs. Carol pacing in circles on his porch. Very odd, he thought; as he opened the door for her to enter and leaned down to kiss her on both cheeks. He greeted her and asked her to excuse his workout odor.

He led her into his family room motioning the
direction with his hands. Ben gently placed his hand on the
center of her back, guiding her until she was seated on his
couch.

"Would you like something to drink?"

"No Benny, I just wanted to come and talk to you,
to see you."

"Sure Mrs. Carol, I'm always here for you. What's
on your mind?"

"It's more like what's on my heart. I don't know if
Camille told you I called her to say I'm sorry. But I did,"

"Yes she told me, I was pleased to hear that you
reached out to her. I would love nothing more than for you
to accept and get to know her."

"Well, I told her she wouldn't be having anymore
troubles with me. I can't begin to say how sorry I am for
attacking you. I just haven't been myself. Never in my right
mind would I hurt you Benny. You have got to believe
me."

"I know that, no need to apologize. It's over let's
move on from that."

"Thank you Benny, you have always been a good
boy, now you are a wonderful man." Mrs. Carol had a look
of bewilderment on her face that caused Benjamin to lean

in to her for a closer view. She had wrinkles on her forehead and a scowl that came out of nowhere.

"Is everything ok?" There was a long pause before Mrs. Carol could speak.

"Do you remember, Lauren? Do you think of her at all? I feel like I'm the only one that feels her absence every day of my life. It causes this ache in the pit of my stomach and my lungs feel as though there is never enough air to breathe. The therapist calls it anxiety and wants me on medicine for it. But it's the fact that I feel her presence every day, but it's her absence that threatens my next breath."

Tears were flowing down her face as she continued. Benjamin grabbed both her hands in his and gave her his undivided attention. "My husband h...her father never wants to talk about her. I just miss her soooo much Benny."

Benjamin moved on the couch near her, forgetting all about his sweaty body. His heart tore for the grief she openly wore. He hugged her and allowed her to rest her head on his chest as he stroked her salt and pepper hair while she cried tears like a river. He spoke gently to this childless mother.

"I remember. I remember our first laughs in junior chorus at church. I remember when I was crushing on her, and how I thought she was the most beautiful girl in the world." Ben chuckled as he continued to stroke her hair. "I remember Tabitha told me she was coming over one Saturday. I brushed my teeth and hair for two hours, trying to look good for Ms. Lauren. I remember exactly when I knew I was in love with her and we confessed our love to each other. Lauren was beautiful on the inside and out. She had a grace and elegance about her that no one could measure up to. I will always remember her; I will never forget. She was a selfless person that gave her time to charities, always helping her friends and family. I know she loved me with all her soul. I regret I didn't love her the way she deserved, or let her go so she could fulfill the role of being a mother and a wife, but she chose who she wanted to love and I'm honored it was me. I know Lauren loved you, Mr. Steele, and me with everything in her. I also know she wants us to live life to the fullest. She wants you Mrs. Carol to look up and live."

Benjamin raised Mrs. Carol's body up so they were eye to eye. "You do know she wouldn't want you to mourn over her this way, right? She wants you to be happy." Mrs. Carol nodded her head emphatically, silently saying yes.

"I know Benny, and I plan on being happy and free from this grief soon."

"That's great. I am proud you are in counseling, continue your therapy and do as Dr. Whitney instructs. We are all here to help you through it. How about I take you to an early dinner?"

"I would love that."

Benjamin got Mrs. Carol something to drink and excused himself to shower. When he was dressed, he took her to her favorite chain cafeteria for dinner. They talked for hours about Lauren, Liberty Fellowship, Camille, and his plans for the future. When Mrs. Carol was leaving his home, Benjamin was hopeful that she was on the path to complete healing. Lauren would want that.

***

*Earlier I.T.S*

"Karen there is no easy way for me to say this, so here it goes, straight with no chaser. A few days before your wedding, my dad asked who your mother was. I told him all that I knew from what you shared with me over the years. He also went through a brief history lesson on how he met Cynthia and shared some intimate moments with her. To make a long story short the lesson ended with us possibly being sisters."

Karen jumped from her seat, furious. Camille could not determine the emotions behind her movement so she stilled in her seat and waited.

"Camille, are you crazy? Do you think that is something you can just spring on me? Hey, Karen my dad said we may be sisters."

"I told you it wasn't easy, but look we are closer than any sisters I know, and the possibility it could be by blood now is just icing on the cake. The fact Nikki could be my niece for real fills me with pride and joy. You tell me this isn't good news."

"I can't tell you that." Karen was now directly in Camille's space. She reached out and pulled her into their first sisterly hug. "It's better than great, it's freaking awesome. I love you like family already."

"Camille? Camille, are you in there?"

Camille was jerked out of her daydream by Debra buzzing in on her phone's intercom." Yes, Debra."

"Legal is on line one."

"Thanks, I will take the call, and tell Karen to come straight to my office when she arrives"

"Yes ma'am.

\*\*\*

It was an hour before Camille was off the conference call with her legal team and the team representing the retailer. They had finally finished their negotiations and signed the contract. She did not mind the length of the call because it concluded with another lucrative account for I.T.S., a multi- year partnership with a nationwide retailer. Camille was elated and proud of her team for pulling together to make it happen.  In addition, she owed Benjamin big time for the referral.  Camille spun around in her office chair, bending her knees so they wouldn't hit the desk. She reminded herself of Nikki when she would come to the office with Tee-Tee.   It was only when she turned completely around did she see Karen already sitting with a look of trepidation on her face.  Did she know? Camille quickly pushed that thought out of her mind. There was no way she knew. She leaped from her chair and rushed to Karen's side.

"Karen what is it? Is it Nikki? Is she okay?" Tears immediately started to flow from Karen's eyes and she just shook her head no, then yes.

Camille was now in a panic "No! Yes! What is it, sweetie, did you find out what caused her episode last night?" Karen lifted her head slowly and began to speak.

"Yes, she has quite a few things food wise and environmental factors she's allergic to. We'll have to monitor her closely and keep an Epi-Pen for her at all times. I picked up one for when she is with you." Camille feeling a little relieved took the allergy list and prescription package Karen pulled from her purse. She glanced over Nikki's restrictions. She was shocked that someone could be allergic to a Redwood Tree, Bermuda grass, but good grief weeds were also on the list. Who knew how to identify weeds? No more trips to the park, and with the length of the tree list, she was thinking about getting rid of her fichus trees in her house that were plastic. The food restrictions, berries, citrus, nuts, and shellfish, was something she wouldn't have a hard time monitoring when she had Nikki. She glanced at Karen again and knew something else was bothering her. "What is wrong with you, talk to me."

"I don't know if I can do this marriage thing with Frankie."

"What? Why not? It's only been a few weeks."

"Yeah, but in those "few weeks" I have had enough of Shayla Jones for a lifetime."

"Are you serious? Why haven't you said anything, what's been happening?"

"I've been trying to deal because we have just been married for a short time." Karen took a deep swallow to collect her thoughts on where to begin. "It started on our honeymoon, Shayla called him constantly. First, it was about the girls wanting to move from Atlanta back home to go to school. Then it was about how they were going to move all their things. Next, it was her momma being sick and in the hospital, he had to comfort her via the phone on our honeymoon, no less. Then this morning while at the doctor with Nikki, she was calling about bank accounts. Oh wait, I didn't mention that, while I was organizing his office with my things I found some of his bank account records. Guess whose name was still on all of them?" Camille didn't think she was supposed to answer that, but apparently was by the look on Karen's face.

"Umm… Sh-Shayla."

"Bingo! We had it out about it and Frankie said he just never thought to take her name off them since they both still supported Dawn and Autumn. He didn't give her traditional alimony but he allowed her to spend as she needed. Can you believe that mess, who does that? I mean, they have a divorce decree, but my God Camille, they still have joint accounts they share, her name is on the deed of the house I just moved me and my daughter into. But the whopper is the account she was calling about today. The one I didn't see the records for. Guess how much is in that one?" Again, Camille was flabbergasted at the information being shoved at her. Gauging Karen's anger the figure couldn't be in the hundreds or mere thousands.

"Twenty-five thousand." Camille said that with a scrunched up face. She thought he was a mail courier; how much could he have?

"Nope my dear friend, six-hundred thousand dollars and Shayla is getting half of it."

"You've got to be kidding me. What does Shayla do to have that much money in an account with him?"

"Please honey, Shayla is a hair stylist. She can barely pay her rent without making withdrawals from Frankie's accounts. Apparently the man I married, not only works for the government delivering mail, he owns a couple of barbershops, a carwash, and is part owner of a strip club in Atlanta. However, none of that is where the 'six-hundred thousand dollars' comes from. That stash comes from when his mother passed. She had several life insurance policies for him and his sister, who lives in Europe by the way. Didn't find out about her until me and Nikki were looking through photo albums."

"Frankie, has a sister? Oh my goodness Karen. But slow down and breathe, let's think about this."

"I am breathing, and think about what? I married a man I know nothing about; he did not clue me in on anything, not his wealth or family. He led me to believe he severed ties with Shayla. I feel like I am his mistress."

"You are not his mistress Karen, you are his wife, cut him some slack. You are newly married; you are going to be finding out a lot of things about one another. The money is a mess, but he is making it right. Besides, it could be worse he could be bankrupt with a mountain of debt." Camille knew that would get a chuckle out of her and it did, Karen actually giggled through her tears. She gently stroked her friends back and tried to give her godly advice. "I know this is a shock, but you told me you knew Frankie loved you. Not only that, I see it. Give it some time. You all have the rest of your lives to get to know one another. Can you honestly say he knows everything about you?"

"No but..."

"No buts Karen, you have to talk this out with him, hear his complete side of it, and understand why he hadn't severed all ties to his ex-wife. He wasn't serious about anyone until you, and you both moved so fast without asking pertinent questions, neither of you have had the time to be completely transparent. He certainly hasn't had the time to cleanse all of the "Shayla" remnants out of his life, but he appears to be making the effort, which is costing him a pretty dime."

Karen was nodding as if she agreed with Camille. She could have been over-reacting, but finding out your husband is not only a mail courier but also an entrepreneur and practically a millionaire, well less three-hundred thousand dollars, was a lot to swallow, let alone digest. Camille had a point. She would get some work done and talk this over with Frankie tonight.

"You are right Camille; I will get to work. That's what you pay me for, right? I will talk to Frankie tonight." Karen stood up and so did Camille and they hugged one another. It wasn't lost upon Camille that it wasn't the sisterly hug she daydreamed about.

"Karen, why don't you have Frankie drop Nikki off at my house so you can have some alone time with your husband. I have her restrictions list and Epi-pen. We should be fine."

"Thank you so much. What would I ever do without you?" Karen's tears were flowing again, as she squeezed Camille's hands tightly. With guilt, settling in the pit of her stomach Camille squeezed back and replied, "You don't have to worry about that, now dry those tears, and let's make this money."

\*\*\*

Autumn was begrudgingly packing her suitcases to go on a last minute trip with her twin sister Dawn. She loved her sister, who she shared the exact DNA with, but this running was starting to get to her. They had already lost college credits transferring from school in Atlanta to Memphis. They told their parents it was so they could be near the family with the addition of Nikki and Karen, which was partially true. Adding in the fact that their mother, Shayla, was not taking their father's new marriage well, it was logical for them to relocate. However, the main reason they left was that Dawn needed to put miles between her and that worthless man, Wilson Buford. He was a basketball star at one of the universities in Atlanta and was predicted to be the number one draft pick in the NBA. However, what the NCAA and Wilson's adoring fans didn't know was he was an abusive, controlling prick who thought Dawn Marie Jones was his property to control. Autumn only needed to see her sister once with bruises on her body from blows given to her by Wilson. Wilson Buford would not be allowed to take out his "stress of remaining the number one draft pick" on her sister. It was worse when his team lost a game, when he fouled out, or when he didn't consume most of sport centers highlights. Whatever did not go *the Great Wilson's* way she assumed landed on Dawn's back and just like his jersey colors; they were black and blue. Dawn said she was overreacting and Wilson did not abuse her, but she thought Dawn was just covering from him. Now they both were in a hurry to make their flight out of the Memphis International Airport. It was for a girl's trip Autumn had planned with a few of their friends after overhearing Dawn on the phone with Wilson, who was attempting to come visit this weekend. Autumn was hoping out of sight, out of mind. She knew what she was doing was deceitful, but this was the only way to get Dawn to stay away from that joker. She was a loyal soul much like their mom and she would not end that train wreck of a relationship. So that was why she was stepping in hoping somehow, some way, Wilson Buford would be out of their lives at least for this weekend. Autumn was also making sacrifices to keep her sister out of harm's way. She had started a romance with Brock Logan, a handsome European law student. She was trying to maintain a long distance relationship with him, but she was feeling him pull away. However, her sister's safety was her first concern, but she was no fool. He would be meeting her on this trip. She had not disclosed to her parents that she was dating outside the African-American race because she felt it was not of importance. If they lasted another month, which would be their one-year anniversary, she would bring him home for dinner, so to speak. She also knew Dawn was going to be furious when she saw Brock.

Autumn was zipping her bag when Dawn strolled into her room dragging her rolling luggage. She looked at her big sister of three and one-half minutes with a sigh. "I don't know why we must do this girl trip this weekend. It's the only weekend Wilson has free for the next six weeks. If I didn't know better, I would believe you planned this Autumn Jade Jones."

"Dawn Marie, please. Why do I have to plan missing that jerk? You should be happy you don't have to endure him."

"Why would you say that? He is my man; I love him to pieces."

"Why would I say that? Because I'm afraid one day his love is going to leave you in pieces." Dawn threw up her hands in defense.

"Autumn, I told you what happened, it was an accident, Wilson would never hurt me, so please don't go there."

Autumn turned around with an incredulous look on her face. "Dawn accident or not, it should have never gotten to that point. Besides, we have been in Memphis who knows if it would have happened again if you were in Atlanta. It is hard to abuse someone via Facetime, but knowing that sucker he is probably poking the heck out of you on Facebook." Dawn laughed out loud.

"Girl you are crazy. Nobody is being abused or poked anywhere. I told you it was an accident that I caused. Wilson would never intentionally hurt me."

"Yeah, right"

"Why do you act like people can't change? Look at daddy."

"First of all, Daddy never laid a hand on mom or us when he was high. Secondly, you do see another woman is reaping the benefits of dad's improvement?"

"Yeah, that hasn't been lost on me, which is another reason we may not need to leave. Mom is not in a good place, she seems to be plotting and scheming as if she may be trying to get back at dad. I don't know what she is capable of and don't want her harming Karen or Nikki."

"Dawn, Mom is all bark with no bite, she will be okay and we will be back on Tuesday. Let's get a move on, our dream trip awaits. Do you have our little blue signs?"

"Yes, they are in my purse."

"Well, let's do this thang."

*** 

Karen was home preparing a nice romantic dinner for Frankie of shrimp scampi, flounder, steamed vegetables, and garlic rolls. She had chilled sparkling cider and put on a light jazz mixed with love songs playlist. She had dressed for the occasion in something revealing for her husband and a pair of six-inch, platform, red bottoms she now knew he could afford. After her talk with Camille and gaining a clearer head throughout the workday, she was feeling better about the situation. She had phoned Frankie and told him she was onboard with him giving the money to Shayla to cut the ties. She also asked if Shayla could get her own health insurance, since she had enough money.

Karen wanted Shayla out of Frankie's wallet. Dawn and Autumn were his daughters and she loved them as her own. She would never interfere with him caring for them. Shayla Jones was a horse of a different color and she must go. Frankie said he would take care of that, and assured her he was in this with her for life. She took her man at his word. As she tasted her scampi sauce, she thought of all the ways she would be rewarding him. Just as a smirk crossed her face, she heard the garage door lift up. Minutes later her dapper husband was walking in the kitchen hugging her from behind and kissing her on the neck.

"Babe, the food smells good and so do you."

Karen giggled as he kissed and nibbled her neck. "Thanks, but you don't. Go wash up, dinner will be ready in fifteen." Frankie gave her a lingering kiss on the lips and scampered to shower and change.

Their romantic dinner started just as Karen had planned. They began by talking about the closure of the joint accounts. Frankie advised Karen she would need to accompany him to the bank to be added to his new accounts, and she readily agreed. Frankie went into depth about his finances. How he had done well in the real estate market, while being a mail courier, and earned a substantial amount of money. He invested well in businesses such as barbershops, clubs, and carwashes.  He continued to deliver mail because he loved the job; it was as simple as that. Karen had started feeling a bit like a hypocrite and opened up more to Frankie about her horrid past. Frankie, to her surprise, said he loved her even more for being able to overcome so much.

After they finished their meal, one of Karen's favorite songs by Anita Baker came on. It fit Karen's mood perfectly. She rose from her chair at the table and lip-synced the lyrics to Frankie. Lyrics that told him, he belonged to her, and she would always be his. She gave him a dance from her exotic days that would make her a thousand dollars in a night.

As Karen swayed sensually with the rhythm of the music, Frankie sat staring in awe of his beautiful wife. He thought he was going to lose her to his past just a few hours ago. Now she danced before him all caramel and creamy, he couldn't wait to devour her. She moved closer and straddled him. Her lip-sync was audible as she quietly sang the words. He had no idea her voice sounded like an angel, but the words she sensually sang in his ear made him know she was a keeper.

"Tell Shayla something baby, I want you to tell her, you belong to me." She murmured. Frankie had no choice but to scoop Karen up and head to their bedroom where they were caught up in the rapture of love.

Anita Baker was still playing through the house audio system afterward. They were snuggling close, watching television and contemplating picking up Nikki, when their bliss came to an end. Frankie had ten missed calls from Shayla and several from both Dawn and Autumn. He knew the girls were out of town on vacation until Tuesday so he did the unthinkable he called Shayla first.  Karen got out of bed and began to dress, deciding she would definitely be picking up Nikki. She jerked away as Frankie tried reaching out to her to pull her near.

Shayla answered on the first ring. "What took you so long to call me back?"

"What is it Shayla?"

"Someone is trying to break into my house!"

"What do you mean someone is trying to break in."

"Just what I said. Are you going to help me or not?"

"Shayla, call 9-1-1, I'm on the way."

Frankie ended the call and got out of bed. He called out to Karen.

"Karen, Shayla is saying someone is trying to break into her house. She could just be tripping. I told her to call 9-1-1. Can we ride through there on our way to get Nikki?"

How could she say no? He wasn't excluding her or trying to rescue Shayla on his own.

"Sure but this woman is certifiable, I mean why is something always happening to her?"

"I don't know honey; let's just go so we can go get our baby girl."

"Are Dawn and Autumn on the way?"

"No, they went on some trip of dreams. You know people be on social media holding those signs up. They joined the young adult version and are out of town."

"Well at least they are enjoying themselves and not dealing with their mom. But I know this one thing, something better be happening over there or she may get to see the other side of Karen Locke-Jones." Frankie didn't respond as he ushered her out of their home and headed toward Shayla's.

Karen opted to stay in Frankie's silver Tundra while he went to check on Shayla. She thought it was best. She was not feeling very patient and if this was some set up to seduce her husband, the former gang banger in her just may come to surface. She pulled out her phone to check in with Camille, but got no answer. Nikki probably had her in the playroom at Ben's house. She moved on to Paige. She needed to fill her in on Nikki's condition and Shayla's antics. Paige answered on the first ring.

*** 

Frankie made it to the entrance of Shayla's apartment and became nervous as all get out. The door was open and a hole was in place where there once had been a knob, he gave it a gentle push and moved slowly inside. What he found startled him, immediately he was stricken with panic. There were sofa pillows thrown all around the living area, shattered glass from the dining room tables, and family pictures were off the wall, broken on the floor. Frankie became sorely afraid of what he might find as he frantically rushed to the back of Shayla's apartment. He called her name repeatedly only to be met by silence as he checked room after room. By the time he made it through the entire apartment, he had only found destruction—no Shayla. He was in a complete frenzy. He searched his mind as he scanned the area over, hoping for a clue of what on earth could have happened here.

Who would do this to Shayla? He thought. Why? Dear God let her be okay! Frankie's mind went to Karen, and he now regretted leaving his wife in the car. He began to run to the front of the apartment so he could get back to

Karen, and call the police in case Shayla did not get a chance to.

He did not have to go far, as soon as he opened the door to leave, there were policemen in uniform.

"Are you Frankie Raymond Jones?" One of them asked.

"Yes I am."

"Frankie Jones, you have been reported for breaking and entering into the home of Shayla Jones and for attempted battery"

Frankie stood in disbelief Shayla had set him up.

\*\*\*

Karen was in the middle of her telephone conversation with Paige when she saw Frankie being escorted by police in what looked like… handcuffs. She abruptly cut Paige off. They had been on the subject of how Shayla had better be happy that they both were trying to live right or she would be getting her behind whooped and cussed out something proper.

"Paige, hush…girl they have Frankie in handcuffs. I have to get out and see what is going on!"

"What, wait? Why would he be in handcuffs? Let me send Kevin down there. Text me the address." Once she saw the address, Paige knew Kevin was close to the area.

Karen could not believe her eyes when she saw Shayla on the sidewalk adjacent to where her husband was being detained by the police. Karen had gone over to inquire about what was happening. Frankie and the officers, assured her he was not under arrest, just being questioned. She was headed back to the truck when she spotted Shayla across the parking lot on the sidewalk. Shayla had the audacity to smirk at her. Karen instantly knew she was correct in not wanting to check on this nonsense. This conniving wretch of a woman had lured them into a trap.

Karen did not just see RED, she saw FIRE. She didn't take deep breaths, she didn't count to ten, she didn't say the serenity prayer like she heard Frankie recite every morning.  Instead, she was on Shayla unaware of how she crossed the parking lot undetected by the cops or her husband.

Before Shayla knew what was coming, she had been hit, and knocked down smoothly by Karen. She began screaming which caused Karen to wrap her left hand around her throat to stop the agonizing screams of the hateful woman. With her free hand, she began hitting

Shayla in her face. A jab to her eye, a jab to her nose; jab after jab until her face was swelling and blood poured from her nose and mouth. All the while Shayla was receiving the worst beating of her life, her arms flapped beside her as she tried to defend herself. She was kicking with all her might. She knew she had underestimated Frankie and Karen. She never thought he would bring his new little wife with him. She wanted to show Frankie he could not just give her money and discard her, like what she went through with him meant nothing. But it was clear now that Karen was from the streets and in a violent trance that could end her life if someone didn't stop this broad. She tried again to free her arms and legs to get this heifer off her but she was outweighed by Karen's anger.

Karen had lost all control of her thoughts and actions, seeing that smirk on Shayla's face under the streetlight, triggered rage that she had buried deep within her soul. Shayla's actions had brought it all out. Karen would beat this disgrace to the female gender to death, before she let her destroy her marriage. That. Would. Not. Be. Happening. She repositioned herself on top of Shayla so her legs could not continue to kick out, and she delivered blows to her stomach. Karen did not come out of her violent trance until she felt herself being lifted in the air.

When she was placed on her feet, she saw it was Kevin. He held her tightly by the wrists as he stopped a cop who had made his way over to the conflict, more than likely to arrest Karen for assault. However, because the officer knew Kevin was an Assistant District Attorney he agreed to let him handle the scene. Kevin asked him not to call in the report but to get paramedics on the scene that would be discreet.

He inspected Karen and saw nothing but reddened knuckles. He could not believe the violence these educated women of God were capable of. Yes, they always had a good reason but for goodness sake, violence was never the answer.

He still had to clear up whatever was going on with Frankie, which he was not sure of because as soon as he got to the scene he saw Karen attacking Frankie's ex-wife. He knew he had to clear it all up and legally as not to jeopardize his career. It was not lost upon him if he didn't get Frankie, and especially Karen, out of this unscathed he would have to answer to Paige. Dealing with an upset Paige was not on his agenda tonight. He calmed Karen down and helped her back into Frankie's truck. Kevin ordered her to stay put until he could bring closure to this mess.

\*\*\*

Camille and Paige were reading Nikki a bedtime story.  It was a classic by Paul Galdone, *The Little Red Hen*. Camille decided to pack up Nikki and return home after Paige called with the events that had taken place with the Joneses. She didn't think Karen and Frankie would be picking her up after the altercation.  Benjamin had gone to the apartment complex as back up support in case Kevin or Frankie needed him.

Nikki who was oblivious to the chaos around her and was in heaven as her Tee-Tee and Aunt Paige took turns being the animals saying, "Not I said the cat, not I said the dog." When the Hen would say she would do it herself, Nikki always chimed in with "And That's Just What she did."

Camille beamed with pride. Nikki was such a smart and beautiful little girl. She didn't think she could love her more, even if she were her own. In addition, *The Little Red Hen* had been her favorite story too when she was a little girl and her Grammy would read it to her every night.

Very much like Nikki was doing now, Camille always chimed in at the, "That's just what she did" part of the story. To her and Nikki alike, that was the highlight of the book. The little hen was independent and that is what Camille desired for all women and men. Everyone should be equipped with the knowledge and tools to provide for themselves if circumstance forced them to. If people knew, they would find Camille's secret hard to believe, but *The Little Red Hen* is why in *In-Transit Systems* had such a generous tuition plan. She wanted every employee to have the education needed to thrive in life. Hopefully, I.T.S. would be around for years to come.

By the time the hen and her chicks were enjoying their cake, Nikki was fast asleep in the bedroom that Camille decorated for her. Camille returned the book to the princess castle bookcase and kissed her niece on the forehead. She dimmed the lights with the remote control, and closed the door after Paige gave Nikki a kiss on the forehead too. The two ladies headed to Camille's kitchen for some hot green tea and to discuss the night's episode regarding Karen.

Camille sipped her hot tea as she listened in amazement to the details Paige was giving regarding Karen.

"It just doesn't make sense to me why Shayla would call Frankie before the police. If I'm here alone and it sounds like somebody is breaking in, I'm dialing 9-1-1, headed out the back door and calling Ben on my way to him." Camille rolled her eyes toward heaven. "Lord what has my sister gotten into?" Camille grimaced at her reference to Karen as her sister and quickly pulled her teacup to her lips to cover her awkwardness. She didn't mean to let the word sister slip, but the longer she knew the more she could feel their blood ties. But Paige did not know they were sisters so she needed to be more careful with her word choices. However, Paige was none the wiser; she had moved her attention to her tea, after swallowing a huge gulp she looked at her teacup as if the secrets of life were written in it.

"Mille, what'd you put in this tea? It is so good."

"Instead of sugar or artificial sweeteners, I added a tablespoon of honey."

"That's right I've got to start doing that, less calories." Paige took another gulp and remembered the topic of their conversation.

"Back to Karen, she has gotten herself into a fatal attraction love triangle. Somebody is going to get hurt. I don't believe for one hot minute her apartment was broken into. Shayla needs her butt kicked."

"Paige, we can't revert to violence; besides why would the cops be there if there was no break-in?"

"I don't know, something in my gut says there is more to this. I guess we'll have to wait and see when they return, but again something doesn't feel right. It's taking too long for Kevin to call me."

"You are right; it doesn't feel right. I hope nothing foul is going on."

"Shayla, better hope nothing foul is going on. I'm trying to stay on this straight and narrow walk and let the spirit lead and guide me. But that Shayla is trouble, and some people and their actions just beg for you to put a foot up their rear end." Paige said, with conviction.

Camille could feel her sincerity and the love Paige held for Karen. However, she could not let that statement of retaliation go unaddressed. She took a deep breath and put on a serious tone with Paige.

"I know you love Karen, and you are protective of everyone you care about. But I care about you, your spiritual journey, and your relationship with Kevin. You are one-hundred percent accurate; people will push us until they hit our hot button. We all have one, but that is when we have to take several deep breaths…pray…chat…burn some incense, call up those prayer warriors, before we go to the place of taking vengeance and violence into our own hands. Our battles are the Lord's and he alone can fight and win them." Camille looked at Paige and was grateful to see her nodding in agreement.

"You are right girl; I just hope everything is okay." Paige gave Camille a mischievous look as a smirk appeared on her face.

"But incense, I won't be burning." They both laughed at that and sat in silence thinking about their friend and her potentially dangerous ordeal. When guilt overtook Camille, she could not remain silent.

"Paige, I can't believe I just gave you that speech when I am lying by omission, I am holding a secret, that is not right."

"Secret, you no! What is it? You pregnant? Girl I can't blame you Ben is so fine."

"Paige, stop! I'm not pregnant. Ben and I haven't made love and won't be until our wedding night."

"Then what secret, would have you looking like you committed murder?"

"Before my dad left the country, he told me Karen might be my sister. The story he told me concerning he and Cynthia Locke—I know she is my sister."

Camille knew Paige would be shocked but the look on her face was indescribable, Paige was looking through her. She looked frozen in horror. The look was so unsettling; it caused Camille to spin around in her seat to see what caused Paige to become a statue. Nikki stood in the kitchen, holding a Shopkin toy in her hand. Camille almost melted into a puddle where she sat, when she saw her bright-eyed, bushy-tailed niece standing behind her. Did she hear?

"Tee-Tee, I am thirsty."

"Uh...Uh...sure baby girl you want water, apple juice, or milk?"

"Apple Juice."

Paige who had now come back to life, stood up to get the apple juice box while trying to process that Camille and Karen could be sisters. When she returned to the table Nikki was in Camille's lap, and she saw the resemblance. How had she missed it? That R.D. James was something else, but Paige would help Camille and Karen get through this, they were all family. As Nikki drank her juice, they sat in silence. Once she was done, Camille tucked her back into bed. Camille headed back to the kitchen to sit and wait for news with Paige. As she walked in that direction, her front door opened and in walked Benjamin, Kevin, Frankie, and Karen.

As Kevin recounted the story, Paige sat in utter shock, especially at how Kevin had to pull Karen off Shayla. Inwardly, she was proud of her girl, but she wouldn't voice it because she was on the path of peace and healing. However, she still felt like Shayla got what she deserved.

She agreed with what Camille stated earlier, 'Vengeance is the Lord,' but oh how sweet it is when the enemy is trampled over by your footsteps.

It was an enormous relief that no charges were being filed against Karen because Kevin had video evidence that she, Shayla the evil, had snuck into the reception room at the Gardens and destroyed Karen's wedding cake.

Frankie had spoken to Kevin when he returned to work after his honeymoon about his concern over the cake incident and it not being a simple mishap. Kevin was sure Frankie brought it up at Karen's insistence.

Nonetheless, Kevin opened a case regarding the incident, and now had the video and a confession from a waiter who Shayla paid two-hundred and fifty dollars to let her in the room. The waiter admitted that he knew it was wrong, but the lure of the cash, that would have taken him two weeks to earn at the Gardens, silenced his conscience. He was fired from the Gardens, and Paige wondered what his conscience was saying to him now.

Kevin said Shayla was screaming bloody murder and to arrest Karen, until he silenced her with that evidence.  Getting Frankie off was just as easy. Shayla, in all her planning, didn't think Frankie would have the voice mails she left claiming someone was breaking in. Turns out Shayla could have been the one arrested but Frankie and

Karen just wanted the night to be over. They told the police officers they would come to the station if they decided to press charges. Paige knew without asking, there would be no charges filed.

After they finished discussing the night's events, everyone said their goodbyes, and departed from Camille's apartment. The ladies agreed to meet up the next day for lunch at Momma Gladys' Restaurant.

## Chapter 5

### Misunderstood

Karen and Nikki were behind schedule and running late to meet Camille and Paige for lunch. Karen and Frankie had stayed up until the early morning hours talking about the state of their marriage, and Shayla's interference in it. It had been an emotional few hours and Karen's spirit was drained. The thought of the conversation from last night in their bedroom caused her eyes to moisten with tears.

*As soon as they tucked Nikki in and left the room, Frankie brought up the night's events. Karen sighed inwardly because she wanted to forget the night had happened. She was dealing with so many different feelings, ranging from remorse and disappointment, to victory. However, it wasn't lost on her that if it had not been for Frankie voicing his concern to Kevin about the wedding cake disaster, and the subsequent investigation, she would be downtown in lock-up. She deeply inhaled and braced herself for the ride this conversation would take them on.*

*Hopefully, she thought, they would be on the same road when it was over.*

*"Babe I'm sorry about what happened tonight, I didn't think Shayla would do something like that." Karen, already losing her calm disposition, slammed the earrings she was taking off into her jewelry box. She turned to Frankie with a look of disgust.*

*Frankie was alarmed by the hateful look displayed on his beauty's face, but the question that came out of her mouth made a tremor run down his body from the top of his head to the soles of his feet.*

*"Did you ever think I would do something like that, Hmm? Black out and brutally beat Shayla to a pulp? Huh, Frankie? Did you think I was capable of something like that?" When Frankie's answer was silence, she continued.*

*"Frankie, it's clear to me that you don't know what a woman scorned is capable of. But I, on the other hand do! I warned you before we went over there that something was up with Shayla. I told you it did not feel right. But because you couldn't let your 'girls' mother' be harmed we walked into a trap. Now I'm trying to rationalize why Shayla, in her demented mind and ways, is acting as if I broke up your marriage to her. I mean seriously you have*

been divorced for years and she is choosing to go all fatal attraction. I can't figure it out, but let me enlighten you on Karen Locke-Jones." She swallowed deeply and rubbed her throbbing hands together. The beating she had given Shayla had left them sore and aching. Tonight had been a reminder of her younger days, days Frankie didn't have full disclosure on.

"Frankie I have a history with a gang in Little Rock, Arkansas. I was in it for years after I ran away from home. I broke a lot of laws, and quite a few bones of other people in the name of my street family. Tonight, I went back to a state of mind, I vowed never to visit again. I went to a place where I took justice into my own hands because someone was trying to hurt my family. When I saw Shayla looking victorious because her little set up appeared to be working, I snapped!" Karen started to pace back and forth as she spoke to Frankie in a tone, he had never heard from her.

"Frankie! I can't do this. I can't be in a relationship that causes me to revert back to those ways. Tonight I behaved in a way…that…that it seems all I've been learning in church meant nothing. It's like my life of prayer didn't exist and every scripture I knew fell by the *wayside. I was back to being a gang banger trying to take out a street rival." Karen paused then took a seat on the bed as her legs were about to give out. She sat next to Frankie, who had just moments earlier, moved from their bedroom's doorway and dropped to the bed to take in her revelations.*

*"Frankie, I want to love you. I want to be with you, but I can't if Shayla is allowed to be a part of your life. She will continue to test us and I will hurt her or worse, hurt myself by trying to escape from anger and pain. I haven't done drugs since I found out I was pregnant with Nikki, but right now a line of coke is screaming my name. I want to answer with a resounding yes and call my supplier. So, while I love you, being tested by the former Mrs. Jones is something I can't have on repeat. I have a daughter—"* *Frankie halted Karen's words as he grabbed her hands and pulled him to her.*

*"We have a daughter, Karen. We, not just you. We aren't ending. You won't have to deal with Shayla. I will handle it. Now that I have you and Nikki in my life—I would be nothing without you. We can go to meetings together, pray, get therapy...we will work on us. You won't turn back to drugs or the streets. I will handle it, I promise*

sweetheart." Frankie attempted to pull her entire body to his, but Karen broke away from him.

"What do you mean, you'll handle it, did you handle tonight?" That stung Frankie's pride but he took it he would not lose her.

"Karen, I admit I was caught off guard, now that I know that Shayla is up to no good, I. Will. Handle. It." Frankie stood up from the bed; he was not about to continue a conversation that had Karen leaving him in it. There would be no end to them. He went over to her closet and pulled out a chemise for her to sleep in. When he exited her closet he saw she had had moved from the bed to her vanity. He put the chemise next to her. She looked down at the top and then up at him, with a look that clearly asked, "What is this for?"

"I am going to run us some bath water so we can get into a calmer place, then we are going to rest. I don't know what you were planning to say or do tonight but we are not separating or ending. I love you, we are family, and I will never put you in another position where you have to defend me or us."

After he had the two-person Jacuzzi tub filled with warm water, and the Coconut Lime bath salts she *purchased from Niquel's Custom Sugar Scrub, he lifted her off the chair and carried her in his arms. He placed her in the tub and slid in behind her. He bathed her and himself. They relaxed and talked for hours. Karen opened up to him about her childhood, gang life, Mario, his death, and the loss of their baby. Frankie seemed to absorb it all and vowed his unwavering love and commitment to their union. Karen decided, during those moments of peace in the bath with Frankie, that this marriage was the right decision. They were family, and she wouldn't allow Shayla or anyone else to make her throw in the towel.*

"Mommy did you hear me?" Karen was pulled from her reverie by Nikki's pleading voice.

"What did you say baby?"

"I said I'm happy Tee-Tee is my real Tee-Tee."

"That's nice, sweetheart. Come on let's get your hair combed and we can meet her and Paige for lunch."

"Okay, but why didn't you tell me?"

"Tell you what?"

"Uggh, Mommy, you not hearing me."

"Nikki, Mommy is sorry, tell me again."

"Tee-Tee was your sister."

"Sweetie, you know mommy and Tee-Tee love each other like sisters, but we are friends. She is your godmother and that's why you call her Tee-Tee. Just like Aunt Paige is your second godmother."

"No, mommy. I heard Tee-Tee tell Aunt Paige that her daddy was your daddy." Karen immediately stopped tying the ribbon on Nikki's hair and bent down eye-level with her. She held both sides of Nikki's arms as she searched her eyes for understanding.

"Nikki, what are you talking about, when did you hear this?"

"Last night, I woke up because I was thirsty. I heard Tee-Tee tell Aunt Paige that her daddy was your daddy." Karen thought to herself that Nikki must have misunderstood, so she went back to tying the ribbon on her hair.

"Honey, we will talk about it when we see Tee-Tee at Momma Gladys' restaurant." Nikki began to jump up and down with joy causing Karen to mess up the bow she was trying to tie. She gave up and put the ribbon back into the barrette box.

"Oooh, mommy we going to Momma Gladys, I love her she is so funny. She is going to make my pancakes smile. But I still wish you had told me about my granddaddy, am I gone meet him when Tee-Tee marry Uncle Ben?"

"We'll talk about it later, sweetie. Let's go we are already late"

"Okay, can I get my Shopkins first?"

"Yes, hurry." Nikki ran off to get her prized possessions. Karen wanted to believe her three-year old daughter had misunderstood the conversation she overheard. In her gut, Karen knew Nikki had understood perfectly. What was with her life?

*** 

"I'm telling you girls, you have to be careful out there with who you're dating.  You two seem to be headed in the right direction but you have to watch them. Pray and watch ain't that what ya'll learning in church?"

Paige who was sipping on her orange juice was tickled pink for Momma Gladys to be on a tirade about dating. She pushed her a little further by asking, with a mischievous smirk so only her eyes appeared over her glass, "Why is that Momma Gladys? You see something in Kevin and Benjamin, Mille and I are missing?"

"Nah, I ain't saying that I'm just saying be careful, because I have seen folks parading they partners, man and woman, woman and man..." She paused to chuckle. "Sometimes it's man and man, woman and women; they be around her acting like they got gold. Only after they get married they find out they really just had glitter."

Camille was so thrown by Momma Gladys's comment the coffee in her mouth came spewing out across the table landing on the side of Paige's face, causing more laughter between the trio. The laughter and conversation went on for several minutes until the door chimed alerting Momma Gladys that customers were entering. They all gasped as it was a busload of what looked to be fifty or more patrons entering the restaurant.

"Well my girls, looks like my break is over, let me put these lazy bones to work around here. Let me know if ya'll need anything, ok."

"Okay." Camille and Paige said in unison still trying to slow their laughter as Momma Gladys walked off barking at her employees to get to work. After the busload of customers entered Camille lit up to see Nikki running toward her.

"Tee-Tee we made it." Camille stood up and started walking to gather her niece in her arms and give her a twirl. However, it was Camille who was left spinning after Nikki made an announcement to the entire restaurant.

"Tee-Tee, tell Momma you and her got the same daddy, she doesn't believe me!"

Just as Camille was trying to balance herself and Nikki, she looked around to see Karen's piercing gaze on her. The only words she could get out of her mouth were, *"Jesus Christ of Nazareth!"*

In Karen's eyes, Camille's response to Nikki's proclamation, coupled with the look of horror she saw on Paige's face, was the answer she needed. She gently took Nikki out of Camille's arms and turned around for the door. Ignoring Nikki's demands to stay and have smiling pancakes and see Momma Gladys; she darted out of the restaurant holding on to a wailing Nikki. The thought she had earlier was the only thing ringing in her mind, what was with her life?

*** 

Camille and Paige entered through the garage of Benjamin's house. Paige had texted both Ben and Kevin when Nikki blurted out the sister secret.  As much as Karen's quick exodus from the restaurant saddened Camille, she was happy they didn't cause a scene in Momma Gladys's restaurant with so many customers there. She was hoping and praying that Frankie would be able to convince Karen to come over to talk about their family issue. She had spoken to him on the phone in the car while Paige was driving them to Ben's. She gave him a brief, but detailed version of when she found out and why she withheld the information from Karen. She could not get a read on how Frankie felt about her actions, but he said he would try to convince his wife to come over to hear her out. She was kicking herself for being a coward and not coming clean about the possibility they could be half-sister's sooner. She truly let fear and selfishness cause her sweet Nikki to have to spill the beans.  She had made a huge mistake in her procrastinating, she felt sick and although Paige was with her, she felt alone. She needed Ben.

Yes, Ben had warned her if she didn't reveal the news to Karen it could turn out badly. However, she knew her man would not give her an *I told you so*, there was no doubt in her mind that he would comfort and encourage her. As she fought back the tears trying to make it to the room he was in, she stopped in her tracks. Ben was standing in the foyer with open arms; all she could do was rush to him and fall into those strong arms and receive the comfort of his love.

Kevin was standing beside Benjamin when the women walked in and he wanted to get more information from Paige on what was going on today. His mind was still trying to process the likelihood of Camille and Karen being sisters. The story Benjamin told left little room for doubt. This group never ceased to baffle him; the amount of drama in their lives was enough to pitch to a network for a reality series. If that didn't work it surely was a book, it would become a best seller even if it had to be self-published. He shook his head as he recounted the last year of drama in this group. There was a simple date to a theater that ended in a hit and run that left Camille hospitalized. Then there was his girlfriend beating up his mother because of an insult and spit, his mail courier was the father of his girl's goddaughter. That same mail courier was a recovering alcoholic and drug abuser who happened to be wealthy and also had a psycho ex-wife. But the best one had to be the beautiful, surprise, engagement party, when Benjamin proposed to Camille, only to have to be rushed to the hospital because his deceased girlfriend's mother gave him a concussion with a skillet. He shook his head thinking all this from a bunch that called themselves Christians.

Kevin was brought out of his thoughts when he realized he would not be getting any answers from Paige. Once he laid eyes on what should have been her smooth, deep, chocolate skin he saw it had been replaced by a shade of gray. Paige was sprinting toward Ben's powder room with one hand cupping her mouth. He followed in hot pursuit to make sure she was okay; when he caught up to her she was leaned over the toilet releasing the contents of her stomach.

He called out to her as he tried to enter the room to assist her, but she used her free hand to motion for him to stay back. He felt useless and wondered what could have caused her to become ill. Was it stress from the day's

drama? Surely she had not gotten food poisoning from
Momma Gladys's cooking, her restaurant always had a
high score from the health inspection office. Nonetheless,
something was up with his girl's health, she had been
throwing up quite a few meals in the last few weeks, and
her energy had been low.  A thought struck him as he
started adding things up. Could she be expecting? If it were
true, it would just add to those episodes that would make
their group, reality television worthy.

He stood outside the powder room wanting to go in
and help his love. Instead, he stayed back with his chest
tightening with each retch from Paige. He was turning
around to go get water for Paige, feeling it might help her,
when he heard her dry heaving and knew she had emptied
her stomach. Camille was already on the job with ginger
ale and crackers in her hand. He was pushed out of the way
by Camille, who went over to rub Paige's back and got her
to drink and eat the crackers. It wasn't lost upon Kevin, that
Camille's help was received graciously versus his.  He just
stood there in awe as her best friend sweetly cared for
Paige.

Watching them made him sure the beef between
Karen and them had to be squashed. These women were

family. He dropped his head in sadness as he remembered that was the reason Karen was upset; *they were family*. Suddenly the images of his mother disowning him for loving Paige came to his mind. He shook it off as best he could, because he could feel his own lunch threatening to rise from his belly. He left the ladies alone and went to find Benjamin. He wanted to know if Frankie was able to convince Karen to come over.

***

Paige and Camille were now in one of Benjamin's guest rooms sitting on the bed. Camille was observing her best friend as she finished her second bottle of ginger ale. When Paige was done, she looked at Camille and blurted out.

"I'm pregnant."

Camille raised an eyebrow giving her best friend a look that said "really?" She laughed. "Duh!"

***

"I don't care what you say Frankie, I'm not going over there." Karen was sitting in the living area on the couch; Frankie was sitting adjacent to her on an ottoman. Nikki was at a playdate. Karen had called a daycare parent when she left the restaurant, it was the only way she could get Nikki to stop crying.

"Karen, don't be like this, what is wrong with talking to Camille? At the very least you will gain some understanding on why she didn't tell you about being her sister." Frankie wanted his wife to go speak with her sister. He didn't like the fact that Camille kept this secret, but after speaking to her on the phone he understood her reluctance, and now he agreed because there was no reasoning with Karen.

"Nothing is wrong with it, but I don't care what her reasons are. So there isn't anything for me to understand. But you should accept the fact that I won't be talking to her again, EVER!"

"Sweetie, you work with her, what are you going to do there? Avoid and ignore your boss?"

"Humph, who said I was going back to work for her? Did you forget I have a rich husband with a few hundred thousand dollars in the bank? I'll be a stay at home mom before I return to be her assistant."

Karen got up and started pacing. She could not believe her life. All this time she had admired and practically worshiped Camille. She made most of her life choices based on Camille's opinions. And to think how awful she felt when Camille had chastised her for sleeping with Frankie before they were married. Finding out she had trusted a fraud was more than disheartening, she felt hurt in the core of her being.

"Karen you don't mean that, we need to go over to Ben's and talk this out. Kevin said the girls are miserable and Paige has become ill and is throwing up."

"Those conniving heifers should be miserable they led me to believe I was their friend. Ha, the joke is on me. All this time I thought Camille was a good friend, a great boss, and a loving godmother. Now I know she is just a terrible sister and a guilty wench, who took pity on her poor, little, bastard sister."

"Honey you don't know that, you are just letting your imagination get away from you." Frankie stood and grabbed his pacing wife's shoulders to calm her. Looking into her eyes, he searched for the reasonable woman who had made his life complete again.

"Sweetie, you have to give Camille a chance to explain, she called me earlier. She realizes she messed up by not telling you, but don't forget who she has been to you over the last few years. You can't just push her out of your and Nikki's life, she loves you both." Frankie was praying to the Lord that he broke through; he thought Karen had been angry about Shayla's episode, but this was something else.

"No, I'm not going over there to hear why she kept this life altering fact from me. You know what; I always wondered how I got placed at Intransit, now I know. Camille probably felt sorry for her poor, little, stripper sister and decided to do some charity work. Boy she really had me going, she put on a quite a show, she should take a bow."

"Karen, are you really quoting Rihanna? You are being ridiculous." Karen spun on her heels and gave him an incredulous look. Frankie knew if looks could kill, he would be a dead man. He lifted both his arms in surrender. "I'm sorry babe I didn't mean to call you ridiculous. I just want you to hear her out."

"Frankie, why are you on her side?" Karen was now in front of him with her arms folded underneath her chest.

"I'm not on her side. I just understand how hard it was for her to tell you. Mr. James dropped this bomb on her when she wasn't fully healed and one event popped off, then another. She didn't want to ruin our wedding or honeymoon, then when we returned Nikki got sick, then the Shayla incident. I believe her when she says the time just wasn't right." Frankie saw his wife's anger lift she seemed to believe Camille's reasons.

"I can't deny a lot has been going on, I'll talk to her. But. It. Won't. Be. Tonight!" Frankie gathered her in his arms and kissed the top of her head.

"I understand, I will call and let them know we won't be coming. What do you want to do?"

"I'm tired Frankie, I just want to go to bed and for you to hold me."

"If that is what you want, sweetheart that is what we will do."

\*\*\*

Camille sat on her bed texting with her dad. She had tried to video chat via her laptop, but he wasn't able to connect. She settled, as usual, to simply converse via text messaging.

*Camille: Daddy I need you to come home.*

*J.D.: Why baby girl, is everything okay? How are you feeling?*

*Camille: Physically I'm fine. On my last check-up, I was cleared of all physical therapy, I am running again. But, I need you to come home because I'm emotionally and mentally not well.*

*J.D.: Why baby girl, are you still on your meds?*

*Camille: Yes, daddy, I am still taking the Prozac and Xanax as the therapist recommends. But there are some situations in life that exceeds the limitations of medicine Daddy. I need you to come home. Karen has found out you are her father and she has shut me out of her life.*

*J.D.: Baby girl I told you about her connection, just so you would know. You shouldn't have let that been revealed to her.*

*Camille: Well daddy it is, and I need you! Please daddy, come home.*

It had been over an hour since she sent the last text to her father, to say she was outraged was an understatement. It was not lost upon her that when she revealed her problems were not physical he went straight to her prescriptions for anxiety and depression. This was the reason no one in her life knew she took them. She kept both prescriptions in vitamin bottles, and everyone assumed that's what they were. Only she, her dad, and her psychiatrist knew she had been on them since she was a teenager.

She was prescribed them after the nightmares of her mother's last days battling cancer continued into her teenage years. She often dreamed of horrid visions of her mother during her last days battling that deadly disease. In her nightmares, she would vividly see the last stages of her mom's life and how the cancer had eaten her from the inside out. The stench of death couldn't be removed from her adolescent sense of smell. She was haunted with vivid images of her mother's skin hanging from her bones, and the scaly look of her skin, that made her face resemble that of a reptile. She grimaced as she could see her mom trying to smile at her, only it was frightening because her teeth no longer fit in the skeletal face the disease had plagued her with. After each nightmare, her days were filled with anxiety attacks until she could not focus, and her grades started to fall. Teachers began to call and report that she had become withdrawn. Those reports prompted her

Grammy to take her to see a psychiatrist who taught her coping skills for the anxiety attacks. Camille still sees Doctor Kendall once a month, another secret she keeps from Benjamin and her friends.

As time dragged on and no word was received from her dad, Camille sat in her bed with tears streaming down her face. She now realized nothing had changed about her daddy. It was obvious his one coping skill had remained— avoidance. That is what he had done after her mom died, he literally ran from her all the way overseas. He left her with her Grammy who showered her with love and affection, but still her father had left the scene. Taking into consideration what he had shared concerning his relationship with Karen's mom, when Cynthia revealed imperfections he ran and never looked back. This angered Camille and she took out her phone to fire off another text, because a Christina Aguilera song playing on her sound system had prompted her, giving her courage.

*Camille: Daddy, say something, cause I'm giving up on you!*

After several long minutes, she knew he was not going to respond. Her father was again abandoning her; she should be able to accept this treatment after all these years. But, why did it still hurt so badly? She chucked the phone with anguish and resentment. Karen just didn't understand what it was like being raised by the Great Jacob Darius James. It was nothing to write home about. Sure, he was there financially but when it came to her first heartbreak, he said, "Did you take your meds?" When she did not make class valedictorian and cried for days because she was one point away, his response was, "Did you take your meds?"

That is how he raised her from a distance, with respect to Grammy, "Take your meds" and move on from anything negative. She however, continued to reach out to him wanting and longing for more. She finally found out how to get more out of him. She became a success; she graduated with her bachelor's magna cum laude, and went on to get her Masters. Now she owns a successful business. He was proud of that, and proud that she had snagged a man with money and morals. She knew he felt she should have just rolled with the happy parts of life and medicate to avoid the pain of any other challenges.

These thoughts made Camille come out of her Christian character. She went to her kitchen cabinet and pulled out a bottle of wine she had been gifted by a client. She poured herself a glass and changed the music on her playlist. She knew this was the time to take her Prozac and pray. However, she knew better than to mix alcohol with her meds. She had not lost all of her common sense; she just opted for the wine and the sounds of rhythm and blues to deal with the depression she could feel coming on.

She deserved this pity party. She queued Nina Simone's "Don't Let Me Be Misunderstood." She drank and drowned her sorrows in the lyrics of the song and Nina's raspy, sultry voice. No scriptures came to her mind, only the fact that in all her do-gooding she was left to blame for hurting her best friend and sister. With that, she decided to put the song on repeat and pulled out a second bottle of wine. While mediating on the lyrics, she was up swaying already in a drunken stupor; at points of the song that she identified with, she raised her glass and slurred a contemptuous "Amen."

At the end of the song, Camille fell onto her kitchen floor's cold tiles and sobbed. She cried out with a voice of despair for the father above to hear her.

Instantly, as if God had dispatched an Angel, her doorbell rang. She prayed it was Karen. She knew it couldn't be Benjamin because he had to go out of state to handle a customer who had a system shut down.

She reluctantly went to the door and opened it, it was indeed an Angel coming to her rescue. It was her future mother- in-law, Ellen. Camille pulled her in and fell

into her arms. Mother Ellen held her tightly with a mother's
love.

***

"Paige, a baby is a miracle; you know I love
you, right? We are getting married." Paige looked up with a
fiery glare. She was staring at her pedicured toes while
Kevin was giving his, 'this is not the end of the world
speech.'

"What do you mean we're getting married, I don't
have ring?"

"Of course you do sweetheart." Kevin immediately
dropped to his knees, reached into his back pocket, and
pulled out a small blue bag. Paige knew the brand and
knew that bag had once been inside a blue box. When
Kevin, pulled a beautiful diamond solitaire ring out of it,
she gasped and covered her face with both hands. Her
emotions bubbled over into tears of shock and tenderness.

"Paige I love you. I know you are the one for me;
there is no one else that can complete me as only you do.
The reason I went to Atlanta was to make my parents aware
that I would be proposing marriage to you. Although, I
have been planning a more romantic setting, now is the

time to become official. Knowing that you have my seed inside of you, forming into someone special like their momma solidifies we are a family. So, Paige Antoinette Richards, will you do me the honor of bearing my name and spending forever with me?"

"Yes! Yes! I will marry you. I love you with all my heart Kevin Anthony Michelson." Kevin scooped her up and twirled her around. The bliss was short lived because Paige started beating his back and pointing at her mouth. She needed to throw up. Kevin placed her down to let her make her way to the bathroom.

Kevin felt like a helpless douche bag for causing her to become nauseated. He remembered that Camille had given her ginger ale and crackers to settle her stomach. He went in of search them. He hummed all the way to the kitchen because she said yes with no resistance. He thought she was going to regress in her personal evolvement, but she didn't, *counseling was working.*

Now that they were officially engaged, he knew they had a lot to work out because they were on a Christian journey and her being pregnant clearly showed they had lost their way a time or two. In addition, he had decided to throw his name in the election for the office of District Attorney. They would have to marry quickly, babies out of wedlock was frowned upon in politics just as it was in the religious sector. Besides, he wanted his son or daughter to be born to parents who were in love and married.

However, none of the issues they could potentially be faced with was enough to prevent him from sending up his own prayers of thanksgiving. Paige had just committed to becoming his wife and he thanked the Lord for it. He made it to the kitchen grabbed the soda and crackers, and made his way back to his bride-to-be. A grin was plastered on his face as he thought; she was also the mother of his child.

## *Chapter 6*
## *I'm Nothing Without You*

Tamala Sykes was on a mission this Sunday morning. Being the lead receptionist and assistant to the counselling staff, she sometimes helped the finance department when they were behind in posting the receipts of the offering and tithes received in the system.

Truth was, supporting Dr. Whitney and the other counselor's needs of the church often left her bored. She was always happy when the finance department called her in to help. What that department didn't know, was that she not only was keying in the receipts, but she also keyed in on her next romantic conquest by the amount that he paid into church.

This past week she had posted the tithes and offering of the Assistant District Attorney, Kevin Michelson. She was blown away by the amount of his tithes; data entering the number made her insides tingle. If that weren't enough the offering amount was more than his tithes, that just sent her entire body into orbit.

Therefore, she was now on a mission, determined to make his acquaintance. She had done her research by watching the sanctuary's security from the past few

Sundays. To watch those videos, she just had to bat her long eyelashes, smile, and wink at Brother George, head of security. Those video feeds equipped her with where the Assistant District Attorney sat, which was always on the same row with that nutcase girlfriend of his. She knew without a doubt that Paige was no match for her; after all, she had read the notes from Paige's sessions. The girl had deep issues from her childhood, issues that a man of Kevin's status shouldn't have to deal with. There were rumors going around the city that he would soon be the next District Attorney and she wanted to be on his arm, during his election campaign.

She had come up with the perfect excuse for appearing in their row. She would tell Paige her appointment needed to be cancelled due to a scheduling conflict, and she wanted her to have the earliest notice possible. She would just tell Dr. Whitney that Paige cancelled.

When she made it to the row, she was excited to see Paige had not arrived. She looked him over; he was a light caramel delight. He was impeccably dressed in a fitted dress shirt that allowed his biceps to be on display, his dark slacks were pressed against lean thighs, and sitting down he looked like a god. She smoothed down her too tight and too short dress, which was inappropriate for church, and entered the row where Kevin was sitting alone. She leaned down over him as he was writing his offering envelope. Tamala knew it was probably another big check to be posted. Oh how she needed a man with connections and one that could provide her with the lifestyle she coveted. She leaned over being sure to let her cleavage appear in his vision.

"Excuse me; you are our city's Assistant District Attorney, Kevin Michelson, correct?" Kevin looked up and was taken aback by the beauty that was leaning over him, pushing her perky mounds toward him. He immediately had to check his wayward thoughts as he stared into her dark eyes. She could easily have been the most beautiful woman he had ever encountered. But, he knew he had the real deal in Paige, add to that she was at home today because their pregnancy had her ill. He reigned in his raging hormones and penetrating gaze and concentrated on the fact this girl was in his personal space, uninvited.

He answered with a sharp and cold tone in his voice. "Yes, I am, how can I help you?" Startled by his terseness, Tamala had to regroup.

"Um, I'm Tamala Sykes, I work for Dr. Whitney and was looking for Paige Richards. I know she is your girlfriend and normally sits with you. Dr. Whitney won't be able to see her this Friday; I just wanted to let her know a week from Friday would be her next appointment."

Kevin felt guilty for slighting the young lady, partially because he knew he did it to avert his attraction to her, she was just trying to do her job.

"Thank you for the information, I'll let Paige know."

"Oh is she not here today?" Tamala wanted to jump for joy but contained her composure, Kevin seemed to be a no nonsense type of guy. Nothing she couldn't work with though.

"No, she won't be able to make it she is feeling under the weather."

"Well I hope she gets to feeling better soon." Tamala knew she didn't give two cents about that ghetto chic's health, but she was trying to gain some footing with the object of her desire.

"Thank you for your concern, I'll let her know you sent your well wishes to her."

Tamala saw an opening for more dialogue and an open seat so she pushed forward. "Since we have just a few minutes until the service starts is it okay if I take this seat?"

Before Kevin could object, he saw Frankie and Karen entering the row. He was hoping they would come this morning and not stay away to avoid Camille. Paige had told him Camille's side and he fully understood it and empathized with them both.

However, the couple behind them drained all the color from his face. He was now white as a ghost and his heart nearly leapt out of his chest.

He stood up as Tamala was making herself comfortable in Paige's normal seat. She was none the wiser to the change in Kevin's demeanor. He rapidly headed toward the couple who was making their way down the aisle.

"Mother...Dad, what are you doing here?"

Julia acted as if they did not have a major falling out weeks ago. She pulled her son into her arms and gave him a kiss on each cheek.

"Son we have come with a peace offering and to share in this worship service with you. Is that okay?"

"Sure Mom, Dad, come have a seat."

Kevin ushered his parents into the row while explaining Paige was ill and wouldn't be attending the service. He ignored the gleam in his mother's eyes when she realized she would not have deal with Paige. He made

introductions to Karen and Frankie, and Miss Tamala
introduced herself as a friend and sister in Christ of their
son. This left Kevin baffled but he shook it off as his
thoughts went to Paige. He hoped she was feeling better
and that this nausea part of pregnancy ended soon. He
couldn't call it morning sickness because it was occurring
throughout the day.  The lights dimmed drawing Kevin out
of his thoughts, the praise and worship team took the stage.
To his surprise, Benjamin was one of the lead soloists. Who
knew his boy could sing like Bryan McKnight?

      Camille could not hold back the tears as Benjamin
led the praise and worship team with his anointed voice,
singing Jason Nelson's, "Nothing Without You." The
lyrics, *in him do I move and have my being, cause I'm
nothing without you*, rang true in her soul.

      Last night, she decided to forfeit her reliance on
God and turned to alcohol and self-pity, all because she
could not face the consequences of her error in not telling
Karen about their family connection. But Glory be to God,
Mother Ellen showed up in the nick of time.

      Her heart swelled with joy as she thought about the
love of her life sending his mother to check on her. That
spoke volumes to the tether that bound them. Even when
they were apart, when she was hurting, he felt it and

provided her with comfort through his mother in his absence.

She was happy to be betrothed to this handsome man, who was now ministering to the saints through the ministry of song. He had sent a dove her way, a messenger of peace and love, which is what Mother Ellen represented in her darkest hour. She couldn't imagine what damage she would have done to herself if Mother Ellen had not shown up.

Mother Ellen held her for half an hour when she entered Camille's apartment. She held her until the wails of despair slowed, she prayed with and for her. She made her coffee to sober her up and then told her not to be too hard on herself. Mother Ellen was filled with compassion as she ministered restoration to Camille.

She had told her, *"We are all human and sometimes we fall down, but the most important thing is that we get back up."*

Her future mother-in-law was the ram in the bush for her. Camille was spiraling into depression because her trigger of abandonment had been ignited with Karen shutting her out and her dad cutting off communication via text.

But the Lord led Ben to send his mother to her aide. Camille was grateful to Mother Ellen, for the patience and love she bestowed upon her. She didn't scold her she just loved on her and ministered words of encouragement. Camille smiled at the thought of Mother Ellen's advice.

*"Camille you have to get down on your knees and have the courage to believe that the Lord will give you strength to overcome whatever comes your way. He does not put more on us then we can bear."*

*Camille repented and then went home with Mother Ellen to spend the night. She did not want to be alone. She slept in her fiancé's childhood bedroom. Being near his mom, where he grew up brought the peace that she needed.*

Now she was standing in the sanctuary with uplifted hands as Benjamin and the praise and worship team repeated the chorus, *I am nothing Lord, I'm nothing without You, I'm nothing without You, I'm nothing without You.*

Karen was also standing on her feet with tears streaking her caramel face. Her husband was by her side, praying that she would allow forgiveness into her heart. He knew the song was referring to people being nothing without Christ. He also knew his wife needed her sister; she would not be complete without working it out. He lifted his hands and worshipped Christ who was the only one with the power to heal sin, sick souls, and repair broken hearts.

Karen had an emotional breakthrough with the lyrics of the song. She lifted her hands in surrender to allow the spirit of the Lord to breathe through her; she wanted him to live inside of her.

She knew, as Ben and the praise and worship team continued to sing this song, there was no way the Lord's glory could rein her in if she didn't forgive her own sister. Christ had allowed her to escape actual crimes against innocent people. Camille had kept a secret that was, in all honesty, not her secret to tell. Her father should have told her, but Camille had always told Karen he was a coward.

Therefore, without any delay, she exited her row and went to the row with her sister and Mother Ellen. She beckoned Camille to join her on the altar. There Camille said she was sorry as the praise and worship team sang "Let Your Glory Reign in Me." Karen accepted Camille's apology and made her own for not being open to hear her. They embraced and sang to each other, *I'm nothing without you, nothing without you.*

Soon the altar was full of family members and friends worshiping together, and holding on to one another. His spirit was lifted. When Benjamin saw his girl embracing her sister, he almost came undone. He held it together and Benjamin looked out onto the packed altar and inwardly gave glory to the Master as he continued to sing to the glory of God.

Pastor Caine, also felt the presence of God and began to minister to each person on the altar. He, along with his staff of elders and missionaries, prayed for every soul that came to the altar, which turned out to be thousands. A formal sermon was not given, because when the Spirit of the Lord is in the temple, you allow it to have its way.

After Church, everyone gave Benjamin praise for his anointed singing, he man-blushed and gave all the glory to God. No one could tell who was more proud Mother Ellen or Camille.

Kevin introduced his parents to the group. Mother Ellen graciously invited them and Tamala to dinner. Tamala was inwardly smiling as she had become joined at the hip with Mrs. Michelson. She was sure she saw something sinister in her eyes every time Paige's named was mentioned. Yes, she beamed internally; Mrs. Michelson's was another way for her to enter into Kevin's world. The Michelson's and Tamala were going to follow

Frankie and Karen, to Mother's Ellen's. Kevin was going to stop by Paige's first to check on her.

\*\*\*

As with every Sunday, after church at Mother Ellen's house was full of life, love, and laughter. She, Tabitha, and Kierra were busy preparing the last of the food. The men were watching sports and the children, including Nikki, were gathered in a room playing video games.

This was what made Mother Ellen's life worth living. However, she did have a concern, Carol was not a church today, she briefly saw Gregory but he seemed to have left early as well. She made a mental note to call and check on the Steele family, if they didn't show for dinner. She was drawn away from her thoughts as she saw that Tabitha and Kierra were speaking to Kevin who appeared to be without Paige.

Tabitha was taking the to-go container from Kevin and was expressing her concern for Paige as Camille had said she was not feeling well. She also told her it was because she was expecting. Tabitha had grown close to Karen and Paige, not as close as she was to her future sister-in-law, but close enough to realize not to let Kevin know she was in the know.

"So Paige, still is not up to coming out?" Tabitha questioned Kevin.

"No she said she needed to rest up for the work week." Kevin pointed at the to-go container Tabitha had collected from him.

"She asked if Mother Ellen could pack her something to go. She can eat it tomorrow for lunch or maybe dinner." Mother Ellen looked over her shoulder with an endearing smile.

"Of course we will send our mom-to-be dinner to go. Be sure to tell her green apples will help settle that nausea she is battling. Many folks don't know that secret. They think crackers and ginger-ale is the way to go, but green apples work faster."

Kevin was stunned speechless as well as Tabitha and Kierra. As an attorney, he knew when to rest his case. He walked over and gave Mother Ellen a kiss on the cheek, as she continued cooking as if she had not just dropped a bomb that exploded all in their faces.

"Thanks Mother Ellen, I will text that to her and let her know. I—I'm going to check on my parents and join the fellas in the den."

"You do that sweetheart; we will yell when dinner is ready."

As soon as he left the kitchen, the ladies burst out into laughter. Kierra went over and hugged her grandmother around the waist saying, "Grandma you too much."

"Child please, the last time I saw Paige I knew she was with child, but every life is planned by God. I know Kevin is going to do the right thing by Paige, so I'm not worried.

Tabitha just shook her head in merriment as she took a batch of Momma Gladys' homemade yeast rolls out of the oven. Momma Gladys had an employee drop them off every Sunday Morning for the Adams' dinner. There was none that could come close to the buttery, mouth watery taste, of Momma Gladys' rolls.

Kevin had to look in several rooms before he found his mom. She was sitting in the formal living room with Tamala, they seemed to be enjoying looking through one of the Adams family's photo album.

Julia sensed her son's presence and looked around him as she smiled, to see if Paige was with him. Kevin made his way over to the duo that chose to isolate themselves from everyone. He found it odd. His mother spoke first.

"Kevin, did Paige join you? I was hoping to speak to her and settle some things like you wanted." He knew she meant to apologize, but it wouldn't be proper etiquette for his mother just to say she was sorry.

"That's good that you want to settle things with her, but she is not well enough to make it, she sends her regards to you and dad." Tamala, one who needed to be the center of attention, chimed in.

"Kevin, did you tell Paige about her appointment change with Dr. Whitney?" This question alarmed Julia and put a look of disdain on Kevin's face.

"Oh well," Tamala thought. She had made an immediate connection with Julia, now she needed to start breaking down her opinion of her son's girlfriend. "What better way to do that then show Paige as mentally unstable?"

"What appointment?" Julia said with what appeared to be real concern. Before Kevin could speak, Miss Sykes provided the answer.

"Oh you didn't know Mrs. Michelson? Paige is in counseling; she has really been through a lot in her life. I am the executive assistant to the counsellors at Liberty and

Paige is a regular." Tamala saw Kevin's eyebrows meet and knew she had gone too far.

"Miss Sykes, aren't you being too liberal with my fiancée's healthcare information?" Kevin was trying to be polite to this beauty, and not cause a scene in Mother Ellen's home, but he could just feel that Tamala and his mother were up to something. *But what? They had just met.*

"I'm sorry. I didn't mean to offend you or Paige." Tamala looked up at Kevin's strong, chiseled face and batted her long eyelashes while placing a hand on his bicep. Kevin jerked away. He couldn't believe her audacity in touching him in such a familiar way.

"Just see that it doesn't happen again." He then looked at his mom. "Are we going to find Dad?"

Julia's mind was too busy reeling over the fiancée announcement to care about Kevin's reprimand to Tamala for insulting Paige. She would have to school the young lady on subtleness if she and Tamala were to succeed in replacing Paige. Julia thought Tamala was much more suitable for her son. However, she had to play nice because her husband had laid down the law in their home, and informed her she had better apologize to their son, if she didn't she was going to be out with nothing. Unbeknownst to her, Judge Michelson had done research on Paige. He started an investigation after the two of them fought. What he discovered was a secret Julia had planned on taking to her grave.

Steven had uncovered the real reason behind Julia's dislike for Paige. He knew that Paige wasn't the real person Julia had an issue with. Paige's mother had been a rival to Julia. They had been in love with the same man, Paige's father. Her heart still fluttered whenever she recalled how Steven cornered her and revealed the evidence against her. She was floored he would go so far as to threaten divorce, but she believed him. The scandal in the file that he presented to her was all the proof Steven needed to shame her for life.

Because of his ultimatum, she was here playing the game and acting excited as Kevin announced to his father, and the entire Adams' clan that he and Paige were engaged and expecting their first child. She didn't see that one coming, and neither did Tamala, but a baby would not abort her mission to get Kevin Michelson.

Camille and Karen were in Benjamin's old bedroom talking about their sisterhood. Camille was so happy that Karen had decided to continue working for her at ITS. After talking everything out and they were going to have a DNA test performed to verify that they were indeed sisters.

Camille suggested if they did turn out to be sisters they should meet with a family therapist. She confided to Karen about her breakdown and alcohol use, and Karen felt guilty for being a factor in it. Both concluded that their dad was a non-factor in their relationship they would both deal with him according to their personal desire.

They were about to call Paige when they heard loud noises from downstairs. They took one look at each other, bolted for the door, and made their way to where the noise came from.

When they arrived, they were excited to see Kevin holding up a tablet with Paige on the screen. Everyone was congratulating her on the baby and pending marriage. They all knew Kevin and Paige were new to the Christian faith, and there was a silent understanding that no judgements would be passed because they were doing the right thing in getting married and having the baby.

After they had disconnected the video chat, Mother Ellen called everyone in for dinner. In the spirit of tradition, Uncle Jack led the prayer and prayed for everyone in the room, the city, the nation, international affairs, he prayed until Benjamin said, "Amen, thanks Uncle Jack for that beautiful prayer."

It was an hour into dinner and most people were on dessert when the doorbell rang. When one of the cousins answered, Mr. Gregory Steele stumbled in calling out for Ellen.

"Where is Ellen, I need her." Mother Ellen heard her best friend's husband's voice as she was rocking Nikki to sleep in her rocking chair. Karen immediately took Nikki from her lap so she could go to Brother Steele.

"Here I am Greg, what's wrong, is Carol all right?" Mother Ellen could see the despair on his face; he appeared to have aged twenty-years since she had seen him this morning. She knew what his answer was, but she had to hear it. So she asked again with a trembling voice.

"Gregory is Carol all right?

"No Ellen she's not. She killed herself this morning while I was at church."

## *Chapter 7*
### *If this is the end*

*3 weeks later*

    Camille was driving in her crimson SUV en-route to Benjamin's. He had called her earlier in the morning and stated they needed to talk. She would be lying to herself if she didn't admit this could be bad news for their future. He had been pulling back since Mrs. Carol's suicide, a suicide that shook the foundation of Liberty Fellowship. Everyone wanted to know why and how could a Church Mother take her own life. Dr. Whitney and her staff were working overtime, administering grief counselling, while they educated the members of the church and the community about the dangers of untreated depression and grief.

    Benjamin, had gone through the motions of being there for Mr. Steele, he was a pallbearer at the funeral, and a soloist at the home going celebration. Camille still was bewildered by why they called it a home going. Does someone who commits suicide have a chance of going to heaven? Camille began to think about going through the motions; Benjamin was definitely doing that in their relationship.

Their wedding was two weeks away and they had completed the marriage counseling, where Benjamin answered the questions as if he had been given the correct answers beforehand. Their time together had been limited because a week after the funeral, Kevin and Paige were married.

Kevin had thrown his proverbial hat into the ring, to run for the District Attorney's office, and he and Paige had to be married quickly. His father Judge Michelson married them at the Michelson's Manor in Atlanta, Georgia. That weekend had been a tough one. Although Paige was now thirteen-weeks along in her pregnancy, her morning sickness had not let up. When it was time to kiss the bride Paige had to run to the restroom to empty her stomach

Camille's mood turned more somber as she thought about the news Paige had just got today from the OBGYN. Some of her prenatal tests were showing early signs that the baby could have sickle-cell anemia. What were the chances of that happening, a biracial father receiving the trait from his African-American mother and Paige having it from one her parents? Paige and Kevin were in good spirits about all things that meant working for the best for their baby's health. Camille was certainly praying it was so.

Truth be told Paige had confided to Camille, Karen, and Tabitha that she was more concerned with Kevin's volunteer staff manager. Tamala Sykes had taken the position, and anyone with eyes could see she intended to take Paige's place. Paige had stated she and Kevin argued over it but she lost because he needed someone fast. Tabitha, who was on the volunteer staff promised to keep her eye on Missus Thang.

As Camille drove, her thoughts drifted to Karen. Their DNA test had come back ninety-nine percent positive that they were siblings. They received the test results from the lab and opened them together in Camille's office. Judging from the jumping, screaming, and tears they both shed, no one would have known there were issues in the beginning when Nikki blurted out the secret. She was happy everything was working out. She still had a bone to pick with her daddy when he came back into town for her wedding, but she would deal with that soon enough. She was just happy to have her sister and nieces in her life. Dawn and Autumn were now just as much her nieces as Nikki. When they returned from their vacation they were livid with Shayla for the stunt she pulled. Neither of them was speaking to their Mom, but there was something else going on with the twins and she knew deep in her gut that was another story to be told.

Camille pulled into Ben's garage and her stomach began churning. She gave herself a pep talk. *He Loves Me, He loves Me.* As a matter of fact, before she got out the car, she put Jill Scott's version on play and listened to it as she deeply inhaled and exhaled. By the end of the song, she was ready to face whatever Benjamin had for her. Deep inside she was wishing he would be standing in the foyer with his arms stretched out wide to embrace her, like he had done so many times in the past.

She did not get her wish; Ben was not in the foyer. She found him sitting in his game room in the dark. He looked so different from the man who cared for her after she was hit by a car and suffered seizures from the brain injury. She looked at this bearded stranger and felt like she was losing a game she never wanted to play.

She had not asked him to sweep her off her feet, in fact she tried to chase him away. She was for the most part content with her life; she had a successful business, great friends, and enjoyed reading her novels. Heck, outside of Paige and Karen, her closest friends were independent authors she supported and her Facebook book clubs. Sure, she wanted to find love and have a family, but the look on Benjamin's face right now, as he stared up at her—a look of doom—was why she stayed away from relationships. At least, if she didn't like the hero in the book she was reading, she could delete it from her reader or just put it on the bookshelf and never open it again. But now, what if this Hero doesn't want her? What if she is not the heroine after all? What if Lauren was *the one* all along and he couldn't love again although he tried to love her? If this was the end, she was of a mind just to make a run for it before he uttered one heartbreaking word. Before she knew it, she was backing up to make her exit. The next then she knew she was running to the garage to escape the hurt.

Benjamin sat in the game room and watched the love of his life assume the inevitable, the end of the relationship. He expected her to be angry and accuse him of being a liar. He was definitely that. He promised her the moon and the stars and could not deliver any of it. Mrs. Carol's suicide made him feel like a murderer, a repeat offender at that. He had accepted his fate of living alone for the rest of his life. He couldn't keep Camille hanging on to hope that their wedding was going to come to pass. He didn't have it in him to spit on Lauren's and now Carol's memory by being happy in love.

However, when Camille started running away from him, his own life flashed before his eyes. One that was dark and filled with empty days and lonely nights. He saw himself alone visiting the tombstones of a woman that never belonged to him and a mother that never let go.

He saw himself witnessing his friends Frankie and Kevin have children and wives that were healthy and happy, while he had memories that were never made.

When he envisioned Camille living that same desolate life because she belonged to him and no other man would ever take his place, something in his heart and mind burst. He was up running after the love of his life.

He ran as fast as his over six-foot frame would allow him and he caught her just as she was about to get into her SUV. He pulled her backwards into his body, as tears flowed from his eyes into her hair; he bent low so he could whisper into her ear.

"I love you Cam, I want us. Help me! The grief and guilt inside me is so great, I am struggling to breathe. I can't breathe" Camille heard his cry and turned to face him in his arms. She wiped the tears from her hero's face, pulled him down to her, and placed a kiss on his lips, she then whispered to him.

"Then breathe through me."

Benjamin and Camille were back in his game room sitting side by side staring into one another's wet eyes. Ben had Camille's hands in his, and squeezed them gently as he tried to work out the lump that had formed in his throat.

Camille could see the anguish in his eyes. She could feel his nervous energy transpiring through the sweat of his palms and brow. Her guy was in a dark place and guilt had him paralyzed. She had an answer for his paralysis. He could move through her as she allowed Christ's strength to move through her…through them. She had received the answer to her question "Was she his missing rib?" She had received a resounding yes when he stopped her from leaving and admitted he was in need. Words were not needed. She would be his rock as he had always been hers. She moved closer, embraced him, and lovingly whispered into his ear Psalm 32:8.

*"The Lord says, 'I will guide you along the best pathway for your life. I will advise you and watch over you.* Benjamin, the Lord loves you and me and he has set us on this path together. I'm not meant to be alone and neither are you. Our path is a united one and I won't be getting off of it. I'm here with you."

Benjamin was overwhelmed with so much joy and relief, that his sorrow lifted at his bride-to-be words. He pulled her closer and they embraced as he stroked her hair and pulled one side behind her ear and spoke directly into it.

"Thank you for not giving up on me babe." Camille crying looked into his eyes.

"I'll never give up on us we weren't built to break."

That night they made an emergency call to Dr. Whitney who came over and counselled the couple. Benjamin was able to open up about his sense of guilt and obligation. Talking about it aloud made his chest expand, lungs open, and he was not only able to inhale but he exhaled.

Later that evening when Camille was home, she got on her knees and said a prayer on behalf of her groom.

"Lord, thank you for Benjamin, that I get the privilege of calling him my future husband. You have spoken over us, changed us, and blessed us. You thrill us, Lord, with all you have done. We will forever sing for joy because of what you have done in our lives (Psalm. 92:4)! Thank you for how You have worked in us. Thank you for giving us another opportunity to trust You more. You are so worthy. You are so sovereign.

"The enemy tried to destroy him with grief and guilt, thank you father for saying NOT SO!

"I am thankful for how you have used Benjamin in my life. Because of His faith in You and his decision to walk in your magnificent light, I am encouraged to follow him hard after You. Thank you for his determination to grow and to seek You with his life. I'm more than willing to trust him with our future family. Give Him strength today, Lord. Give him the wife he needs in me. In Jesus's name Amen!"

\*\*\*

Mr. & Mrs. Benjamin George Adams stood at the entrance of Liberty's opulent, fellowship banquet hall receiving their guests as they entered to celebrate their nuptials.

Benjamin was having a hard time focusing on greeting the guests because Camille looked more beautiful than ever. When the doors of the sanctuary had opened to

Kirk Franklin's "Now Behold the Lamb," his bride was the truth and light of his life.

Over the last two weeks, she had been more than a help to him, their family, and friends. As usual with their group, obstacles were always coming their way. Karen and Mr. James had a meeting that went completely left and Camille had to ask her father to leave her office before things got out of hand.

Paige's pregnancy was becoming worse while Kevin's campaign demands picked up. Kevin was stressed because of the baby's potential health issues and that Paige was unhappy with his choice of Tamala Sykes being on his staff. Benjamin exercised his right to plead the fifth on that topic.

Dawn and Autumn, introduced boyfriends that had Frankie and the rest of the adults doing double takes. Then there was his mom and Gregory Steele, getting too close after Mrs. Carol's death. Nonetheless, his girl was by his side every day for grief counseling, all while holding down their family, friends, and her business.

As the reception line came to an end, he was able to guide his bride to their table and help her take a seat. He leaned over and gave her a movie-ending kiss on the lips, and inwardly thanked the man above for finding his good thing.

**Author Notes**

I am thrilled to have presented *After Church* to you. I hope that one of the characters resonated with you. For me, a little bit of myself is in each one of them. Like everyone else, situations occur in my life, some that come with pressure and I'm up against the wall. It is during those times that I have to decide, will I allow the Holy Spirit to lead and guide me? Or will I go with my emotions and barrel over anyone or anything that threatens my peace? My answer is—we all fall short of the Glory of God from time to time. It's important that we not dwell in our shortcomings but press toward the prize of a higher calling in Christ Jesus.

It is imperative that we move forward from past hurt, and not let our failures rule our future. The character, Mrs. Carol Steele, could not move forward from the loss of her daughter, Lauren. She loved Lauren and refused to heal from her grief. Her grief manifested in her angry actions against others and vicious words she spurred to the innocent. Mrs. Carol was depressed and never recovered.

Depression is real, it must be treated, and the patients suffering from it must do the work to become better. This is a personal testimony of mine. I'm not ashamed to say, I have a therapist along with prayer and the

Word of God. Don't let your loved one suffer, know the signs and help them.

It is my prayer that you were inspired and entertained by the characters of *The Greatest Love Series.* I would love to hear from you, see my contact information below. Until we read again, I pray that you are blessed.

Genevieve

Coming Next

Dawn and Autumn: Finding Him!

The Greatest Love Series Books

Book 1 All I'll Ever Ask

gdwoodsbooks club recommends

Faith -Her Love Story

Contact me: gdwoods75@comcast.net

Like my Facebook Page

Visit my website

Please visit the following sites for more information on the following:

Chronic hives disease

http://www.mayoclinic.org/diseases-conditions/chronic-hives/basics/definition/CON-20031634

Dating and Domestic Violence

Love is Respect

Call 1-866-331-9474, chat at loveisrespect.org or text "loveis" to 22522, any time, 24/7/365

Suicide Prevention

Suicide Prevention 1-800-273-TALK (8255)

## Book Club Questions

1. Do you think Paige and Kevin married to soon?

2. Do you think Tamala will succeed in her quest to get Kevin?

3. What do you think of the sudden closeness of Mother Ellen and Lauren's Father?

4. Do you think Shayla will ever get over Frankie and let him and Karen be in peace?

5. Do you think Paige and Kevin will have a healthy baby?  Will Kevin's mother ever accept Paige? If not, how will it affect their marriage?

6. Do you think the deaths of Lauren and Mrs. Carol will continue to haunt Ben?

7. Do you think Karen will ever be able to forgive her father for not being a part of her life?

8. Do you think Kevin and Paige will find out that their mothers loved the same man?

9. Do think Dawn's relationship is abusive? What do you think will be the outcome?

10. How do you think the family reacted to Autumn dating outside of her race?